LOOKING BEYOND THE GUILT

A NEVER-ENDING TRAIL

DRISH KING

To my mom, Dr. Sonia Kochhar for spending an hour to come up with the perfect title for my book...

Contents

Contents

Preface

Writing in the Crime genre is a wild experience because your mind has the freedom to throw in betrayals, twists, and dark pasts as it pleases. It is a billion times more enjoyable when the crime book is part of an ongoing series because you are already familiar with the characters and have the full freedom to play around with the plot.

However, it turns it hard as well because you need to keep the initial essence of the characters alive and similar throughout numerous books yet show their character development.

This precarious and tedious task requires countless hours of you pulling at your hair while sitting in front of a blank document. At times, your fingers don't seem fast enough to jot down the thoughts flashing through your mind, and at other times, you find your mind completely drained of any ideas.

The same happened to me while writing this book. I was either writing three chapters in a day or not writing more than one line in three long months.

One thing about creativity is that it cannot be predicted or scheduled. You need to let it flow at its own pace. The best ideas will always come to you at extremely inconvenient times like sitting in an examination hall and you will conjure up only overdone and mundane ideas when you are sitting in front of your laptop. The trick is to let it all flow without criticism and to welcome the irregular flow of ideas to cherish their full wave.

You need to go easy on yourself and allow yourself to play around with the plot of the story because you can't choose the best route for your story without exploring every narrow street with a dead end.

Writing can be overwhelming, stressful and even burdening at times but above all, it is freeing. It frees you from the burden of carrying an untold story and somehow for the writer...that's all that matters.

So, here I bring you the thrilling third book in The Guilty Series, introducing 'Looking Beyond The Guilt: A Never-ending Trail' that upholds the legacy left behind by 'Guilty Or Not...?: Secrets Of A Wanted Criminal' and 'Guilt Unfolds: The Ghoul Of His Past'.

This book of the series is brimming with betrayals, tragic pasts, and wicked plots that will make your head spin and this book would not be a part of The Guilty Series if it didn't have the never-ending sass and humor of Hannah Gorgin.

So, buckle up for this adventure that will take you to the extremes. I hope you have got some tissues by your side because it is going to be nothing less than an emotional rollercoaster.

Prologue

3 Years Before ------------

Every single citizen was asleep on that fateful night, except a guilty soul who was talking in hushed whispers over the phone and a deceived one who had just jerked awake due to a peculiar feeling of being betrayed even in that lonely night.

She kept on twisting and turning in her bed but couldn't shake off the weird sensation that was haunting her dreams.

Finally giving up on recharging her energy for her new case, she got up and tip-toed outside her room, only to find the man she knew very well or someone she *thought* she knew very well having a hushed conversation while lurking in the darkness of the drawing room.

His low voice flowed through the melancholy air into the ears of the woman he had wished to keep shielded from the conversation, "I am trying, trust me...But she is the best fit for this...I *need* her to protect Anna...just for a while, I promise...After that everything will return to what it was five years ago...She alone can clear my name...Don't worry...I am planning...It's gonna be over soon..."

She shivered from head to toe but her shiver had nothing to do with the cold outside because the icy suspicion was freezing her heart, eating her out from the inside...

However, as she went back to bed and gradually slipped into a dream, she decided to blame the weird hallucination on her sleep deprived state.

Little did she know, life was trying to prepare her to face the most brutal betrayal she had ever came across...

"Please wake up, Han..."

A soft sob could be heard from a room, its entrance hidden by the bookshelves of a house. A green-eyed man was sitting on the floor, holding a rather pale-looking hand of a woman which was covered with bandages and a drip. Her chest heaved up and down in a slow steady rhythm that was perfectly in sync with the monitor attached to her, sitting on the side of her bed.

The man's misty eyes stared into space while his hands were busy rubbing the unconscious woman's cold knuckles.

"Han, Anna is not eating anything without you forcing food into her mouth..." He let out a hollow laugh, "...Frank wants you to wake up so bad that he is consulting more and more doctors while keeping your identity hidden...And I...I miss you. I have no idea what to do without you...without you telling me it is all going to be alright...without you telling me that...that we will get through this together..." His voice trembled at the end.

Fresh tears trickled down his cheek and some landed on the woman's hand, "So, you are not going to wake up today as well? Fine. Just remember that...that I will not talk to you for a week after you wake up if you keep this up"

He paused as if waiting for her to reply and then continued helplessly, "I know you are doing this to avoid my rebuking after the stunt you pulled there at the hospital. I...I won't complain. I won't do anything. Just...Just wake up..."

He broke down completely. He kissed the back of her hand and entangled their fingers, placing her hand on his chest and keeping it there for a while.

He would have stayed there forever, weeping for ages, if a voice hadn't broken the mournful silence engulfing him, "Dad, where are you?"

He frantically wiped his tears and said firmly and steadily, "Just checking on mom, Anna. Do you need something?"

"It's been an hour, Dad. I'll watch over Mom if you want. You need some rest," Anna screamed from the other room, her voice seemed to be getting nearer with every word.

The man took an uneven breath and said, "Coming"

He tucked a stray piece of hair behind the woman's ear, kissed her forehead with trembling lips, and went outside the room quickly before his daughter could enter and see his broken and messed up state.

Only if he had waited one more moment, he might have noticed the slight beep of the monitor and the faint twitch of the woman's hand where his tears had fallen or if he had been lucky enough...he might have even heard her faint whisper, "Soovin..."

A hooded man was leaning in a chair. He sighed deeply and lazily, stretched his hands that were covered with a blood-thirsty rotting ghoul's tattoo, and settled peacefully in his chair once again.

Another man entered the room brimming with uncertainty, "You called, Captain?"

"Any updates on Hannah Gorgin?" The seated man asked without any excitement.

"Not yet, Captain. She has not been spotted anywhere till now. So, we believe that she is still in a coma"

He leaned back in his chair, deeply in thought, and muttered to himself, "We *believe*...It's been a month..."

A smirk crept on his lips as he sat forward in his chair, "I have so many plans for her but this girl just doesn't want to get up...I am getting bored...How is Soovin doing?"

"He has disappeared from the outer world and spends all his time inside the house"

"Doing what?"

"We...We don't know, Captain"

He turned to look at him with cold contempt, "Then, why are you alive?"

"I...Captain...We are working on it-"

"Five minutes is all you have," he cut him off.

The man fumbled with his phone and dialed some numbers, engaging in quick and crisp conversations frantically while his master chanted monotonously, "Tik...tok...tik...tok"

"He has not stepped out of the house in forever but in a store, one of our men overheard a conversation between the man and girl who were with him. They were talking about him and how he spends the entire day alone in front of a computer doing god knows what"

His eyes shot up as the guy's words caught his attention, "Frank and Anna..." He muttered under his breath, "Oh, old friend...What are you up to...?"

"Shall I go, Cap-"

"Are they still living in the same house?" He cut him off.

"We saw the man and the girl returning to the same house"

He smirked evilly, "I think Hannah might need a little help getting up...Perhaps a little surprise...Do one thing"

"Yes, Captain?"

His smirk widened, "Send a little gift to them"

Heavy tired footsteps echoed off the walls and filled the empty silence. A blond man with ocean-blue eyes stepped inside the room. His lingering gaze settled on the computer in front of which was sitting another man.

The man was sitting in front of the computer with tired, emerald-green eyes. Although the large dark circles beneath his eyes suggested that he hadn't slept in ages, his eyes were wide open and his fingers quick on the keyboard.

The man who had just entered the room shook his head in disappointment and muttered, "Soovin..."

The man on the computer looked up with a jolt, his hand already reaching for the gun in front of him, but he relaxed on seeing those familiar ocean-blue eyes.

"Frank..." He said, "Did the doctor say anything about Han's condition?"

Frank said sympathetically, "No...How many times will you ask me the same question...?"

Soovin gulped, swallowing his tears, and returned his attention to the computer he had spent numerous hours on.

Frank sighed with a tinge of sadness, "Soovin, why are you watching the exit footage again?"

"You know"

"But I don't understand"

"You never will"

"Make me, then!" He said, frustrated.

Soovin looked him dead in the eye with his cold orbs, "I want that man who dared to lay a finger on her"

"This is madness!" He threw his hands in the air.

"I told you...you will never understand," He shrugged and returned to his computer.

"Soovin, just think about Anna. She needs you"

"I..." A stray tear trickled down his cheek, "Just...Just leave me alone for a bit, Frank...Please"

"*A bit?* You have been alone since Hannah was shot and that was almost a month ago!"

"And she still hasn't woken up..." Soovin muttered as fresh tears threatened to spill.

Silence unfurled in the room.

After a while Frank whispered gently, "Soovin...You miss her, don't you...?"

Soovin just stared at his screen, not trusting himself to answer without sobbing.

All he could mutter was, "I..."

"Look," Frank sat down on the chair beside him, "I miss her too. She was my sister for heaven's sake! I want her to wake up as badly as you but you can't let go of all your responsibilities. Anna has not been any better. Making her eat anything is a struggle in itself"

Soovin remained as quiet as the calm before the storm.

"You need to leave your obsession with finding this man and concentrate on GG. I have a feeling he is planning something horrible"

"He can't take anything else away from me, I...I have already lost everything"

Frank leaned forward and looked into his eyes, "We both know he can, Soovin. This...this is not what Hannah would have wished for if she was awake"

"I..." He let in a shuddering breath, "It was my fault. All my fault. I should've listened to you. I...I killed her"

"No, you didn't, Soovin. Listen-"

"I broke my promise...I couldn't take care of her..."

"Soovin, you-"

"Only if I had not driven rashly in a frenzy to get her to the hospital...Her brain wouldn't have been injured...I *killed* her..."

"SHE IS NOT DEAD! She...She can't be," Frank broke down as well.

Suddenly, a small girl came running into the room.

"Anna," Soovin reached for her as she struggled to speak in between breaths.

After what felt like ages, she finally panted, "I saw...Mom...The monitors...She is waking up"

CHAPTER ONE

BACK IN BUSINESS

I was tied to a chair with a ghoul-tattooed hand holding a gun pointed at my forehead.

"You made a grave mistake," GG growled, "And now, it's time for payback"

All I could feel was hopelessness as he pressed the trigger.

I awaited the excruciating pain I was all too familiar with but it never came and the scene around me melted into another.

Soovin was standing in front of me.

He whispered teary-eyed, "I am sorry, Han" before pointing a gun at me.

"Soovin," I whispered, feeling betrayed and shocked beyond measure, "I thought you-"

He pressed the trigger just like GG had and I could feel my conscience travel to another world, some other dimension.

I am dreaming, I realized, *But then, why am I unable to wake up? Also, if I am aware of my dreaming state, am I even asleep?*

I tried to gain control of my mind, to remember the last thing that happened to me but all my brain could muster up was a billion scenarios of me dying miserably...alone...betrayed...grieved...helpless...

This is not me, I tried to tell my brain, *GET UP!*

But as soon as I became sure that I was not in reality, my mind would melt away and yet another horrifying scene would resurface.

I could see Anna, standing alone, dejected and crying. She was running away from someone. I could see her distress but I couldn't do anything. I tried reaching out to her but I couldn't even feel my body. It was as if I was watching her as a mere spectator while my body was somewhere else.

"MOM!?" She was crying out, calling to me, helplessness evident in her voice.

I wanted to answer her desperate call, tell her that I was there, but I couldn't. My senses seemed frozen. I could only feel emotions, no sensations.

Then, a hand reached out, the one with a familiar ghoul's tattoo and a gun. The gun's barrel was aimed at Anna. Then, the hand pressed the trigger.

I opened my eyes with a jolt and broke into a cold sweat. My breathing was ragged and my movement restricted as if my body rejected all my demands to move.

I could feel an oxygen mask strapped tightly to my mouth. I gripped the sheet of my bed tightly as terror clutched my heart.

I was lying on a bed with various hospital machines attached to me. My eyes darted around and I saw an asleep Soovin sitting on the floor with his upper body leaning over the bed. He was clutching my hand firmly as if his life depended on it.

The horrible sight made my heart writhe. He appeared devastatingly pale and fragile. There were big dark circles under his eyes. His face seemed to lack any liveliness. This wasn't the Soovin I knew.

I tried to call out to him, "Soovin..."

I felt his hand suddenly squeeze mine and heard one of the machines urgent beep before my surroundings melted away and I was again transported into a world of nightmares.

Then, it hit me. The bullet in my stomach. Soovin driving the car. The excruciating pain. His teary-eyed expression. My trembling blood-stained hand on his cheek. Then, I had gone blank...I WAS IN A COMA!

Before I could process anything else, I was greeted with yet another nightmare.

Frank was lying unconscious somewhere that I didn't know. His entire body was damp with his blood. His ocean-blue eyes had become lifeless orbs floating in a void. I wanted to cry out but my voice seemed trapped somewhere miles away from my mind.

Then, the tattoo on Soovin's arm resurfaced in my mind, jerking me awake. My body had responded to the surge of adrenaline.

I was in reality once again. I saw Frank and Anna on either side of me. Both of them were staring into space.

"When will she get up?" Anna's voice echoed in the empty room.

"I...I don't know, Anna," Frank said, his voice thick with tears.

Before I could show a single sign of movement, the darkness engulfed me once again.

It was GG, the hooded man I had arrested all those years ago on that fateful night. He was standing upright among three dead bodies - Frank, Anna, and Soovin.

I tried to clench my eyes shut.

The problem?

My eyes were already shut. This horrifying picture was going on inside my mind. But every cloud has a silver lining. I could feel my despair slowly fight the dreamy state I was trapped in.

Then, GG barked out a laugh that sent shivers down my spine.

My senses were half-awakened by this new wave of terror.

I could hear a familiar sob tearing through all the noise of GG's hysteria.

It was Soovin's heartbroken voice, "Please wake up, Han..."

I knew it was him. Not some weird hallucination my sick mind had conjured up. It was really him. I could tell.

"Anna is not eating anything without you forcing food down her throat..." Soovin's hollow laugh surfaced over all other sounds from my nightmare, "...Frank wants you to wake up so bad that he is consulting more and more doctors while keeping your identity hidden...And I...I miss you. I have no idea what to do without you...without you telling me it is all going to be alright...without you telling me that...that we will get through this together..."

The way his voice trembled at the end felt like a sharp jab to my heart. He seemed so...broken.

I could feel a drop of water falling on my hand. He was crying. My senses were becoming stronger. I was giving my coma a tough fight.

He continued as I struggled to fight the darkness threatening to engulf me again and held on to his voice as if it anchored me to reality, "So, you are not going to wake up today as well? Fine. Just remember that...that I will not talk to you for a week after you wake up if you keep this going"

It was getting harder and harder to hold on to reality but I was not the type to give up so easily, "I know you are doing this to avoid my rebuking after the stunt you pulled there at the hospital. I...I won't complain. I won't do anything. Just...Just wake up..."

Despite half my senses being in a deep sleep, I could feel a tear trickle down my cheek.

I felt him kiss the back of my hand and wrap his fingers around mine. His warmth was sending numerous sensations to my brain. I knew it was real. I knew I needed to get up but my body wasn't very keen on cooperating.

I felt him tuck a stray hair behind my ear and his warm lips pressing a gentle kiss to my forehead before the warmth vanished as if he was leaving.

No, I wanted to scream, *Don't leave!*

My strong desire reached the tip of my finger and my hand twitched. I could barely hear my feeble whisper, "Soovin..."

But he walked away. There was no point in getting up anymore...

My body twitched, *Don't listen to the voice, Han. They all need you. You need to get up.*

Then, the darkness came again but this time, I was ready to fight it. I knew this was an illusion. I just had to break through it.

I gathered every shred of strength left in my body; the strength that seemed frozen somewhere. Using it, I fought the dizziness and the void engulfing me.

COME ON, GORGIN! YOU NEED TO GET UP, I told myself as I felt the darkness press over me but I didn't bend. I could feel it strain and my strength slowly unfreezing.

My eyes shot open and my entire body jolted forwards. I began breathing heavily.

I was barely aware of Anna running out of the room for I was way too busy trying to stay conscious. It was proving to be nearly impossible.

Then, when I was at the edge of losing consciousness and giving in to the darkness, I saw Soovin's face and heard his scream, "HAN!?"

Frank and Anna were at his heels.

Seeing all of them, I knew I had to get up. It was as if they had pulled me from the brink of a cliff leading to my doom.

My vision cleared and my senses started returning at a snail's pace.

But another wave of darkness combined with dizziness hit me and I would have given in if Soovin hadn't grabbed me by the shoulders. The simple contact was sending a hundred sensations to my brain, keeping it rooted to reality.

He was trying to keep me in the moment.

Turns out, I wasn't the only one with in-depth knowledge of coma. However, Soovin must have studied about it while my knowledge came from some pretty nasty first-hand experience. Lucky guy.

"HANNAH!?" All their screams were mixed and my brain wasn't functional enough to distinguish them yet.

So, I decided to concentrate on the only thing I could - Breathing.

I was panting. I could feel my heart pumping inside my chest. My hands were no longer lying lifeless on the side of the bed but were clutching my oxygen mask tightly for dear life.

Soovin was rubbing circles on my back while trying frantically to stabilize my breathing. Taking every single breath seemed like a massive task. My brain was craving oxygen and I knew that if the demand wasn't met, going back into an even worse coma was the *best-case scenario.* The worst being becoming brain-dead.

My survival instincts kicked in and I tore the oxygen mask off my face, throwing it on the floor.

I started taking deep breaths but my brain seemed to need way more oxygen. My head was starting to get dizzy and my eyelids felt like they were made of lead. I was about to lose consciousness but Anna's anxious voice, Frank's hopeful sobs, and Soovin's desperate words of encouragement kept me going.

Soovin gestured for Frank to clear the way for some air to reach my poor lungs. He helped me calm my breathing and I could feel my senses coming back to me. He was still rubbing my back while Anna rushed to get some water and Frank rushed outside saying, "I'LL CALL THE DOCTOR!"

I leaned back towards Soovin's familiar warmth as my nerves calmed down a bit.

My lingering gaze met his anxious one and I made the brave effort to try for a confident smile.

It took all my strength to say, "Guess who made it back?"

He placed his warm hand on my cheek and smiled.

A tear slipped from his eyes as he replied in a trembling voice, "A ferocious fighter"

CHAPTER TWO

A Short-Lived Reunion

The past moments were still a blur for me. I was aware of the three of them watching me intently with concern and hope but I was struggling to get my thoughts straight.

My head was swimming. I felt like my brain was defrosting. Every single sense of mine was entangled in a mess. I could feel that mess slowly resolve and my senses returning to me but not fast enough. I was dying to feel like myself again and had the urge to bang my head on the wall if that was what it took to regain my composure.

"She is in post-coma state," I heard Frank say, "Her senses would be pretty messed up right now"

I muttered, "Tell me about it"

From my half-open eyes, I could make out him smiling faintly. That brought a smile to my face as well. My growing serotonin and dopamine levels were accelerating the comeback of my senses.

After a solid minute of me trying not to collapse again, I opened my eyes wide enough for my eyeballs to fall out.

"Han, are you good...?" Soovin asked in a fragile voice.

I tried to sit a bit upright. Soovin decided to help me after I nearly managed to knock myself out once again.

I smiled at him, "As good as I will ever be"

At that moment, Anna crashed into me and hugged me tightly.

I chuckled lightly and hugged her back, "How are you doing, little one?"

She sobbed in reply, "I...I had been waiting for you to..."

I rubbed her back in a comforting manner while eyeing Frank and Soovin playfully, "Well...at least *someone* missed me"

Before I knew it, I was engulfed by both those giants as well and I could barely breathe.

Pro tip: Getting sandwiched between three people right after you wake up from a coma is *not a good idea.*

I smiled at the thought, *I sure am coming back to my regular self.*

I could hear all of them sobbing in relief and feel their strong grips over me. I smiled weakly and after god knows how long, I felt at home once again.

I had no idea for how long we all stayed like that but my arms were pretty heavy when we finally separated.

Frank wiped tears from his face and said frantically, "You little-Do you know what-"

"Chill, blondie!" I grinned despite my body's protests, "I am fine. Besides, you look horrible. Have you forgotten how to sleep?"

He shook his head and muttered, "You try sleeping when your sister is fighting for her last breath..."

I sighed out dejectedly when I heard how broken he sounded, "I am sorry...I...I should have-"

"Told me about that damned bullet a bit earlier!" Soovin eyed me threateningly but I could see the tears of relief that he was holding back.

I turned to him, "I..." My gaze softened when I saw his horrible state, "Soovin, when was the last time you slept...?"

He looked hither and thither as if he had been caught red-handed and said dismissively, "That's not important-"

"He has not slept since you went into a coma," Anna said, her face still buried in the crook of my neck.

I looked at him accusingly, "Really? It was what, like a week ago?"

Frank gulped uncertainly at my words, earning a questioning look from me.

Then, he said in a soft voice, "Han...You have been in a coma for a month"

"A MONTH!?" I was pretty sure my jaw was touching the floor.

"You are kidding, right?" I asked in disbelief.

"I wish he was," Soovin said in a low voice.

"But...a month...?" I had no idea how to process this new information, "How-"

"Okay, that is enough," I heard a new voice say from the door, "This is the patient, I suppose?"

I turned towards the raspy voice and found myself staring at a man with a doctor's coat over his shoulders and a stethoscope hanging from his neck.

He had a dark complexion and an oval face. His jet-black eyes were staring at me, not with sympathy or interest but with...a dark emotion that I could not decipher properly, thanks to the post-coma state of my mind.

He declared, "The patient needs time to cope. I recommend leaving her alone-"

"Doc, I think I am good," I interrupted.

He raised an eyebrow at me, "I am pretty sure you are still finding your senses intermingled, Miss"

"No, I am getting a hang of it," I shrugged, "Besides, we don't have much time-"

"Han," Frank glowered at me, "You'll do as the doctor says"

I threw my hands in the air which was a bad idea as it sent pain rushing through my body, "OH COME ON! I have done medical training as well-"

"Are you a coma specialist?" Frank said, "Because I don't think so"

I stared back with a look similar to his, trying to win this battle.

Some of the curious minds might be wondering why I was arguing so much about such a simple matter.

The doctor was giving me a bad vibe.

I have no idea why but my first instinct was to knock him out cold and I was still waiting for the day when my sixth sense would be proved wrong. I was pretty sure things were about to go down in a really ugly way if I didn't attack him right now.

That can be a post-coma thing, my brain seemed to say but I had learnt the hard way *never* to ignore my gut feeling *ever*.

However, Frank didn't seem to budge, "You are just delaying your treatment, Han"

I sighed and turned to Soovin. His piercing gaze saw right through me. The weary and relieved look on his face was replaced by a frown and a look of suspicion laced with confusion.

He probably understood what I was trying to tell him.

This doctor is bad news, I wanted to scream.

He came by my side and placed a reassuring hand on my shoulder.

"Doc," he turned towards the doctor, "Is it fine if I stay here with her?"

The doctor eyed him suspiciously, "Well, it can result in-"

He cut him off, "Because it is recommended by the WHO to have a friend or relative near the patient who has just woken from a coma to calm the patient if he or she gets puzzled or frantic"

He raised his eyebrows, "You lot seem to know an awful lot about coma"

"Medical students," Frank said frantically and shot us a what-on-earth-are-you-guys-up-to look.

"Well," The doctor said, "You are right young man but this is a special case-"

"I. Am. Staying. Here," He said with a tone of finality and his grip on me tightened. I had no words to express how much that simple action reassured me.

The doctor kept on arguing, "This might-"

"Just a second, doc," Frank approached us and whisper-shouted, "What are you guys doing?"

Soovin sighed and whispered his reply, "Look, I know I messed up the first time. I couldn't take care of her-"

"Soovin," Frank shook his head, "If you say that you broke your promise one more time, I am going to knock your head off. We will have this conversation later. For now, let's-"

"I am staying, Frank. It's...It's not going to happen again...I am not making the same mistake again. Besides," he smiled, "Someone needs to be here to make sure she won't pull any stunts or threaten the poor doctor to declare her fit so she can jump in front of the dangers once again. You know how your sister gets!"

"Hey!" I complained and jabbed my elbow into his ribs.

Frank smiled, "Well, I agree with you on the last part. Just...Stop blaming yourself, okay?"

Soovin nodded half-heartedly.

Frank turned to the doctor, "Well, doctor. Hannah, the patient is a black belt in a number of martial arts and she is kind of short-tempered and impulsive. So, Soovin would stay here to make sure she doesn't...pull any stunts. The coma has messed up her sense of judgement a lot you know..."

The doctor sighed defeatedly and nodded, "Fine"

Meanwhile, Anna's steely gaze was aimed at us and demanding the truth. I made a conscious effort to ignore it. It was extremely difficult.

"I'll call you both in when I am done with the checkups," He told Frank and Anna and they both left the room.

The doctor turned towards me and the way he looked at me sent a shiver down my spine. Things were about to go south fast and I was damn sure of it.

Soovin whispered in my ear, "It's fine, Han. Just relax...You can't think straight right now. It's nothing, okay?"

Oh how much I would have loved to believe him but I knew better.

The coma could have messed up my sense of judgement but I had trained myself pretty hard not to go against my gut feeling.

I looked at him and nodded passively.

The doctor approached me with a syringe and I could have sworn I saw him smirk or maybe I was hallucinating...?

I knew that I couldn't trust my sense right now but what else did I have to rely upon?

"It's just a pain killer. Now that you have woken up, even though the bullet wound on your stomach is healed, it will start to sting soon," He readied the injection.

I eyed it suspiciously.

If it was just a painkiller why were the hair on my neck standing up by glancing at the injection? Surely, that couldn't be blamed on my wrecked coma as well.

I squinted. I had served in the CIA for seven years and the five years after that weren't free of bullet and knife wounds but never in my entire life had I seen a painkiller like that.

I thought miserably, *If only I could read the-*

"Doc, if you don't mind, can I have a look at the labelling?" Soovin asked, reading my thoughts as usual.

The doctor raised an eyebrow and I saw his fingers clutch the medication vial tighter, "For?"

"For...my studies," Soovin cooked up another lie, "It would *really* help me because in my years of...*study*, I have come across a million painkillers but...this one looks a bit unfamiliar. Would you please allow me to read the labelling?"

I noticed the doctor's forehead cover with beads of sweat but his body language didn't appear to be frightened at all.

He shrugged casually but didn't hand Soovin the medication vial, "It's a new anaesthesia painkiller"

I narrowed my eyes, "Why anaesthesia instead of Analgesia, may I ask? Because I don't feel like a loss of consciousness is needed right now"

"*I* feel so, Miss. Need I remind you who is the doctor? And if you must know," He said in a confident and matter-of-fact voice, "Your...brother, I suppose? told me about your bullet wounds and coma in some detail and I suspect that it would have gotten worse and would require immediate surgery"

I opened my mouth to argue but he cut me off with a sympathetic smile, "Look, I know what you are going through. I have no idea how you, a medical student as you claim to be, got a bullet wound like this but I assume it wasn't all sunshine and rainbows. After whatever incident left you like this and your post-coma state, it is perfectly normal to be suspicious of even your doctor"

Soovin gave me a reassuring look as if realizing that I might have been feeling suspicious and paranoid because of my state and not because of some Sherlock-level intuitions.

A small cough escaped my lips.

Soovin reached towards the side table to pour me some water.

The doctor chuckled while flicking his finger at the medication vial, "I have dealt with pretty suspicious patients in my career. You won't believe how many worse patients I have treated! The number runs in hundreds!"

Soovin stopped dead in his tracks and dropped the glass of water from his hands in shock, the sound of which made me flinch.

He swiftly turned to face the doctor with wildness evident in his eyes, "Hundreds of patients...? Frank had said that due to such short notice...Only a novice doctor was available..."

CHAPTER THREE

SOMEONE FINALLY SLEEPS

A lot happened in a moment.

The doctor or rather, the man who claimed to be a doctor leaped towards me with the injection held like a knife.

Yeah, he was *definitely* not a doctor.

Unable to move, a big thanks to my post-coma state for that, I helplessly held my hands in front of me.

Soovin leaped towards the false doctor and wrestled him to the ground. Although he was doing great, it was pretty obvious that he needed some help. The man was trying his best to inject whatever was in the syringe into Soovin if not me and the injection was dangerously close to Soovin's arm.

Now, I would love to tell you that I forgot all about my dizziness and jumped into action, heroically saving everyone as usual but the truth is that it took me a solid minute and my entire concentration to get up from the bed without anyone's help.

They both were rolling on the floor and the injection's direction flickered between them. Then, the man said something to Soovin but it was not loud enough for me to hear.

He froze for a second, taken by surprise and that was all the man needed. He kicked Soovin's chest and lunged at me with his injection ready to cut into my skin.

The injection was a mere centimetre away from my eyes.

With a swift movement, Soovin grabbed the man and forced the injection to be injected into him instead.

The sleeve of the doctor's coat slid up a bit in the process and there was that wrecked tattoo that had haunted nearly every nightmare of mine.

I tumbled back into the bed as a wave of shock and dizziness hit me. I could feel my grasp on reality loosen.

Soovin reached for me, "HAN!"

Meanwhile, I was preoccupied with fighting this new wave of coma.

Soovin took my hand in his and placed his soft palm on my cheek.

He knelt on the floor so that we were at eye level and said in a quivering and frail voice, "Hey, I am here. Han, you can't go into a coma again...Please"

Although the world was swimming for me, I could hear the tears in his voice clearly.

I tightened my grip on his hand, trying my best to stay in the present.

He squeezed my hand even tighter in return and joined our foreheads, "Come on...Stay with me..."

My breathing sped up and I found myself struggling to stay awake while panting.

"Copy my breathing..." He whispered softly but couldn't keep the panic from his voice.

He started taking deep breaths and I tried my best to do the same.

Soon, the moment passed and my light headedness faded.

"I think I am good now," I whispered gingerly, not wanting to break the beautiful moment.

I opened my eyes and saw tears shimmering in his green orbs. I gently pulled him to sit on the bed instead of squatting on the floor.

"You..." He took in a trembling breath, "You get a thrill by scaring me like that, do you...?"

I reached for his face while shaking my head slowly.

Up close, he looked even more horrible. I could see his sunken eyes and pale face more precisely than ever. He seemed to be holding in a lot of emotions, emotions that were breaking him inside.

A tear rolled down my cheek as well, "Soovin..."

I placed my hand on his neck and softly pulled him towards me. He leaned in with only a little hesitation at first and then, settled his face in the crook of my neck comfortably, just like Anna had done.

I could feel his hot tears on my neck. He was trembling and weeping quietly in my arms.

After some hesitation, he lifted his arms and embraced me snugly, his grip was protective as if he was scared that I would vanish into thin air if he let go of me for even a second.

I breathed in his intoxicating smell. My heartbeat skyrocketed and settled again. My stomach was a mosh pit yet I enjoyed the peculiar feeling.

I lifted my arm and rubbed soothing circles on his back with one hand while the other was busy messing around and playing with his hair.

"I...I thought you...I couldn't forgive myself...I-" He sobbed.

"Shh..." I whispered softly and hugged him tighter, "It's fine...I am here..."

I had never seen him cry before. He had always appeared as strong as a mountain to me but at that moment, he seemed so delicate that I had the urge to wrap him in my arms and protect him from the entire world.

Soon, his sobs became less violent and his voice didn't tremble as much when he said, "When you were in a coma...Anna was so upset and lost-"

"And she wouldn't eat anything without me forcing food down her throat," I supplied while running my fingers through his hair and gently massaging his scalp.

He broke the hug and looked into my eyes but none of us made any effort to move our hands from around each other.

"You heard me...?" He said with his eyes fixated at mine.

I nodded gently and murmured without breaking our eye contact, "Sometimes"

Finally, I couldn't stand his messed-up appearance anymore.

I said as I continued running my fingers through his messed-up hair, "Soovin...What have you done to yourself...?"

"I..." He no longer held my gaze and looked down delinquently, "I was just...not fine...I..."

I pulled him in a cozy hug once again. He didn't show even a flicker of hesitation this time instead, he settled in my arms like a bird in its nest.

His familiar snugness hit me again and calmed all my senses. The feeling of being coated in his warmth made my eyelids heavy and gave me the urge to sleep peacefully.

I felt him inhale deeply in contentment and had to fight the urge to pull him even closer as if I wasn't crushing his bones yet.

He muttered in a soft voice, "I am not saying that I missed you but...I would have appreciated it if you would have woken up a bit sooner..."

I pulled him closer which was somehow still possible, partly so that he couldn't see the crimson color spreading in my cheeks. Meanwhile, my mind was busy going haywire.

I felt him chuckle lightly, "You look cute when you are trying not to blush..."

I suddenly found the off-white wall incredibly interesting but when he shifted to get closer to me, I couldn't help but mutter, "You are an adorable idiot..."

It was his turn to silently struggle with blushing but I could see the back of his neck and the tips of his ears turn red.

"You sleeping a little wouldn't have affected my chances of waking up, you know?" I whispered, mainly to change the subject.

I could feel him sigh against my neck. The sensation sent sparks throughout my body.

"I tried...Nightmares...Horrible ones...They just wouldn't let me sleep"

"Can you sleep now...?" I asked softly.

I felt his hot breath on my skin as he let out another sigh, "I don't want to let go..."

"I didn't tell you to," I said while my mind was busy melting at his every word. My stomach had already turned into a wild zoo.

I sat a bit straighter as Soovin leaned towards me more. He secured his grip over me which turned my knees to jelly.

I bent forward and pressed a soft kiss to his forehead. He smiled at my gesture and snuggled closer to me like a toddler.

"I missed you, Han..." He said in a sleepy voice.

"I missed you too..." I whispered.

Soon, I felt his breathing slow down. A moment later, the steady breathing had turned to soft and silent snores.

I admired his relaxed face for a while before I felt my eyelids getting heavy. After all, waking up from a coma and being jump scared by a so-called 'doctor' right after wasn't a walk in the park.

Within five minutes, I was dozing off with Soovin in my arms.

Thank god for the wonderful timing or else I would have encountered a panicked Frank and Anna rushing to the room because they found the real doctor's unconscious body at the gate of the house. I might have even seen the terrified and puzzled look on their faces when they saw the intruder lying unconscious on the floor.

Who knows?

If I had been awake for one more moment, I might have seen Frank's knowing smirk and Anna's mischievous one, maybe even heard Frank mutter in Anna's ear, "Let's give them some space, shall we?"

CHAPTER FOUR

YET ANOTHER ATOM BOMB

I woke up and sighed in bliss. No nightmares. No tattooed hand sneaking up on me. Not even any grave danger. Just a dreamless sleep.

God, you finally showered some mercy upon me!

I opened my eyes a fraction, trying to adjust to the blinding light of the room.

My lingering gaze settled on Soovin who was wrapped around me and an involuntary smile made its way to my lips. He was sound asleep as he should be after so many sleepless nights.

Suddenly, my calm was replaced by panic as I remembered the intruder. My eyes frantically searched for him on the floor and then, in the room.

It was then, my feverish gaze landed on two bowls of fruits kept on the table. My stomach grumbled in protest. My eyebrows shot up when I saw a note next to the bowls.

I reached for the note carefully and reluctantly. Carefully because Soovin needed some more sleep and reluctantly because my experience with notes had not been great.

It was in Frank's handwriting - 'Fruits for you both tired and sleep-deprived souls. After eating them, come to the living room or my room if I am not there. Don't worry, I took care of our not-so-friendly doctor and fed a bunch of lies to the real one so that there is no space for any suspicions. The underappreciated genius under this roof, Frank'

My immediate thought was, *TRAP, TRAP, TRAP!*

I flipped the note and on its backside was written - 'PS: Not everything is a trap, Han. But if you are still not convinced, (5,4) (5, 3) (2, 4) (7, 5) (9, 4) ~ (3, 4) (2, 4) (7, 3) (3, 4) ~ (3, 4) (2, 4) (5, 4) (4, 3)'

I closed my eyes and recalled the image of a keyboard to decipher the code.

It was our safe sentence- 'FRANK SAYS SAFE'

I smiled and took my bowl.

We had developed this peculiar code language to communicate with each other in case we needed to prove our identity to the other.

However, if we got into the exact details and rules of our unique code, we would be here for ages. So, let's continue with the story.

I started eating the fruit and made a mental note to make Soovin learn that code as well. With GG hovering over us like a dark shadow, it could come in pretty handy.

GG.

With that, my thoughts shifted to the quagmire we were stuck in. My mind refused to believe that GG had given up on us. I knew it in my heart that he was not done messing with our lives. The *doctor* he had sent was an open testimony to this.

Had he done or at least *tried* to do something while I was lying on the bed for a month?

Surely, my mind seemed to reply, *He wouldn't hang around and wait for you to wake up, would he? He is GG for God's sake!*

I smiled at my thoughts. I was back in form and the CIA Officer within me was more than ready to pounce on him like a hungry lion.

Time to get back on track, I thought, *Start where you left off.*

I closed my eyes and concentrated as flashbacks flooded my mind.

Then, it clicked.

Alex. I had stuffed him in the car before I got shot. Surely, Frank and Soovin would have interrogated him to get to the bottom of this, right? They had *a month*. That was more than enough time for a simple interrogation.

I recalled their appearances when I had woken up.

Boy, who was I kidding? They had been in no shape to investigate. They had been way too busy crying their eyes out for me.

So, Alex is a potential starting point.

We also had the intruder who had claimed to be a doctor...or did we...?

My eyes darted to the floor where he had been injected with whatever he was trying to inject in me. The medication vial of the so-called anaesthesia lay empty on the floor.

My mind burned with curiosity.

I placed my now empty bowl back on the side table and carefully detangled myself from Soovin's embrace. Then, I quietly replaced myself with a pillow in his arms and got up from the bed.

My head was a lot less dizzy now and my fingers were itching to investigate something, *anything* at this point.

I warily picked up the medication vial and squinted to read the small print.

Propofol.

Yeah, it was a strong anaesthesia. He would be knocked out cold for anywhere between 2 to 24 hours.

My mind was bubbling with possibilities. He probably wanted to kidnap me but not kill me. Of course, how could GG give that honor to someone else?

Wait, did he know I was awake? Probably not as then, he wouldn't have sent just one of his men.

After a while of thinking, I came to the conclusion that this man was probably sent here to check on me and update GG on my situation to launch a solid attack or he was sent to attack Frank and Soovin. He must have realized what was going on and decided to take me as a gift for his dear Boss.

I sighed, lost in thought, *Being taken to GG while in a coma is the last thing I want right now. Who knows the things he had planned for us, especially when he was given a month to do his devious plotting, assuming he had taken a short break while I was out of the game? Let's not find that out right now.*

I heard the creak of the door. Someone was opening the door extremely slowly and sneakily. That triggered the intruder alert in my brain and I automatically reached for my gun.

The problem?

It was not with me. I mentally cursed and took a stance to launch into an attack. That black belt in martial arts wasn't a waste after all.

I dropped my stance on seeing Frank poking his head inside. He did a double take on seeing me standing in a fighting stance not long after waking up from a coma.

"You are awake?" He whispered and gently closed the door behind him, not making a sound.

"No," I replied sassily and smiled.

He rolled his eyes at me and returned the favour.

"Why on Earth were you sneaking through the door like that?" I kept my volume low as well for Soovn's sake.

"Well," He smirked and eyed me playfully, "I didn't want to intrude on you both, you know? I wanted you and him to have your *quality time* in peace"

I scowled at him and smacked his arm hard.

"What?" He acted innocent.

"Shut up," I hissed, "You very well know what"

"Damn, your strength has returned for sure," He groaned while rubbing his arm.

"Oh, you bet," I smirked.

"So..." he wiggled his eyebrows, "Had a good sleep, ha?"

"I *hate* you," I narrowed my eyes at him, trying my best to ignore how much my cheeks were burning and instead focus on the medication vial in my hands.

Frank's eyebrows shot up, "Really, Han? Back on track again?"

"God knows what GG is up to. He isn't the type to give us our sweet time settling down now, is he? The little gift he sent makes that pretty clear. We don't have time to lose," I replied curtly.

"Not even for some teasing and brother-sister moments?" He asked hopefully.

That brought a smile to my face, "Later, blondie. We have things to take care of"

He lowered his voice, "Be honest with me. I am your brother; I know when you are lying. Han...What *exactly* do you think about Soovin?"

"Shut up for Jesus's sake!" I looked away to hide the fact that I was redder than a tomato.

"Mind you, I am not letting this go," He smiled knowingly, making me facepalm to hide my crimson face.

"Can we *please* have a serious conversation now?" I said with my face still hidden.

"Whatever," he smirked for the last time, "Anyway, that fake doctor guy is out cold but he is still breathing. What the heck did you do to him?"

I briefed him on what happened with the intruder, leaving the later part out of how Soovin and I ended up asleep on each other.

"And then?" Frank probed smiling.

"And then, I kick you in your damn face," I said exasperated.

He shrugged and muttered, "It was worth a shot. Did you figure out what was in that vial?"

"Propofol. The fake doctor won't bother us for a while"

"Any idea who sent him?"

"You haven't checked his forearm, have you?"

His eyes widened in realization and he kicked the floor in frustration, "Of course it was him! That wrecked GG"

"What did he do when I was...you know?"

Frank rubbed his neck and said uncertainly, "Nothing...?"

I raised my eyebrows, "For real?"

"Ya," He answered, "I mean...nothing that we know of"

"He is planning something horrible," I muttered.

"I believe that too. This was the first attack since the hospital one where his men tried to turn off mom's ventilator"

My heart sank as I recalled it.

I asked in a weak voice, "How is mom?"

Frank narrowed his eyes in displeasure and muttered, "About that..."

"Frank," I didn't even try to hide the panic in my voice, "How is she...?"

"Well, there is good news and bad news"

I flinched. *Bad news.*

He read my expression, "The *good news* is that mom's security is tighter than ever. Two dozen CIA Officers are guarding her now. Even GG can't lay a finger on her"

My eyes narrowed in suspicion, "Why?"

"Well..." He shifted uncomfortably, "That brings us to the bad news. But just remember that it led to the good news and so the result was-"

"Frank," I cut him off as my heartbeat touched the sky, "What happened?"

"Umm...Well...you were spotted at the hospital, so..."

"Will you be direct for once?"

He threw his hands in the air, "You should not receive shocks! You might go into a coma again"

"I promise I won't. Now, TELL ME!"

He took a deep breath as if mentally preparing himself to get this over with.

And that my friends, is how I got my second shock of the day that nearly sent me to coma again.

He clenched his eyes shut and said in a single breath, "Mom has gone in a coma and you have been charged with an attempt to murder her"

"WHAT!?"

And I mean it when I say that my scream could probably be heard up to Mr. Dune's soundproof office in the CIA headquarters.

CHAPTER FIVE

MULTIPLE SCREW UPS

There was a loud thud right after my scream. I turned around to locate the source of the sound and noticed Soovin lying on the floor, trying to adjust to the sudden brightness while screaming unintelligent nonsense.

Frank exclaimed joyfully behind my back, "You didn't go into a coma again! Woah-Soovin, are you fine, buddy?"

Meanwhile, Soovin was busy having a panic attack of his own, "What happened? Han, are you okay? Is GG here? Are we under attack? Is it-"

"Calm down! Everything is fine," I tried to reassure him.

He gave me a skeptical look, "Really? You scream like *that* when everything is fine?"

All my shock and anger exploded, "IT'S NOT *MY* FAULT-"

"She just got to know about her recent charges," Frank cut me off.

"Oh..." Soovin made a sympathetic face while getting up.

He looked at me and made a horrible attempt to calm me down, "Well...It's you who said that one page added to our overflooded file and 57 cases instead of 56 wouldn't make any difference. So, I don't think 58 cases would cause any inconvenience either"

I took a step towards him with the intention of strangling him. Luckily for Soovin, Frank stepped between us just in time.

He exclaimed, "Really, Soovin? *That's* how you calm Hannah down? Honestly, how will you two live together after you both-?"

I and Soovin simultaneously stepped over Frank's foot rather harshly, making him jump in the air like a kangaroo.

"FINE!" He exclaimed, "I wasn't saying anything!"

I think I heard him mutter something along the lines of, 'Man, I am going to get sandwiched between these delusional idiots'

"What was that?" Soovin asked.

"Nothing! Just nothing," Frank wrung his hands, "So, where were we? Ya, Han, so Mom's security is tighter than anyone right now. No need to worry about that"

"What about her condition...?" I asked teary-eyed.

Frank sighed gloomily, "Wel...She has gone in a coma...but the doctor says she'll get up any day now"

"He has been saying that since we admitted her..." I muttered dejectedly.

Soovin changed the subject, "Let's worry about things that *are* in our control, shall we?" He turned to Frank, "What about that fake doctor-"

Frank cut him off by handing him his bowl of fruits.

Soovin looked at the bowl as if it had come from another planet and shot Frank a look that said what-on-earth-do-you-want-me-to-do?

"Eat," Frank instructed.

Soovin opened his mouth to protest but Frank held up his hand to stop him.

"Eat while we figure things out or Hannah here would not hesitate before knocking your head off because she knows it's for your own good"

"It would be a pleasure," I smirked at Soovin who gulped after being at the receiving end of my look and put a piece of watermelon in his mouth, munching on it quietly.

"Damn, Han..." Frank muttered, "Literally everyone is terrified of you, even your-"

A jab of elbow right between the ribs did the job of shutting him up quite effectively.

"If I ever get a broken rib, you are paying for my surgery," He groaned while rubbing his ribs.

"What about Alex?" I asked as the sudden question popped into my mind again, "We had brought him in the car, right?"

Soovin avoided my gaze while Frank stared at the floor.

"Where is Alex?" I repeated, a bit louder this time.

Frank flinched, "Look, Han, that was not one of my proudest moments"

Soovin nodded, "Ya, not at all"

I eyed them suspiciously and said in a threatening way, "Where. Is. Alex?"

Frank gulped, "I suppose I have to take the credit for this"

Soovin raised his eyebrows, "I think you mean blame"

"Okay, now I am getting curious *and* agitated," I said.

"Okay," Frank sighed, "So, after taking proper care of you, we turned to Alex and gave him some more anaesthesia to buy us some time to settle things down. Then, we had kept him as a hostage. Turns out he was pretty annoyed after being trapped here once again. He tried to escape like two days ago...but your brave brother gave it his best! I fought so valiantly-"

I cut him off, "You can just say he escaped again instead of beating around the bush, you know? It's...not even that bad. We had already extracted all the information from him. Now that I am already considered a murderer, what harm will getting accused of being a hostage-taker as well do? We just have to change our location so that the CIA doesn't ambush us"

"Oh, I took care of that," Frank waved his hand dismissively, "I thought that GG might tip the CIA anytime. So, now, the CIA thinks that you and Soovin have left Anna to me and that little girl doesn't know anything. Plus, the entrance to this room and the adjoining rooms is hidden by some bookshelves and stuff. No one knows about these hidden rooms. I did say I was an ace at house planning, didn't I?"

"Great!" My eyes lit up, "Then, it was a pretty good thing that he escaped. After all, he was just an innocent misguided child. He deserved to go free"

"Hold your horse for a bit, Han. You didn't let Frank finish," Soovin said while casting a you-called-this-upon-yourself look to Frank.

"Well," Frank said while nervously rubbing his neck, "I *stopped* him from escaping. But...in the process...I had to keep him trapped somewhere and...he was struggling quite a lot and he hit my head with something...while I was trapping him. So...I trapped him in some sort of daze and I...I have no idea where I kept him"

I opened my mouth to say something but then closed it when my mind failed to comprehend a proper response to the uncoherent nonsense I had just heard.

I never thought this day would ever come but, I was indeed left speechless.

"In short, he lost Alex the day before yesterday," Soovin said.

"How..." I struggled to find the right words, "How can you *lose a breathing human being?"*

"Frank is pretty talented if you look at it that way," Soovin muttered under his breath but none of us laughed.

Frank just stared at the floor guiltily while I stared at him threateningly.

"So...you are telling me that Alex is hidden somewhere in this house, counting his last breaths when he wasn't even the one at fault...?"

I took his silence for a yes.

"Oh good lord..." I muttered and buried my face in my hands, "Frank...you *really* screwed up in the most creative and peculiar way, didn't you?"

"Yeah...I kind of did..." He said sheepishly as the tips of his ears turned red.

"And you can't find him?" I looked up.

"Nope," He said as if he had lost a toy he had borrowed from me and not a literal human who would probably die now.

"Are you sure you have looked everywhere?" My voice sounded helpless and weak even to me.

"I have myself searched every nook and cranny," Frank said, "Not a soul"

Soovin suggested with a shrug, "He is pretty well-trained. Maybe he will find a way out by himself?"

None of us replied.

I sighed out, "I suppose I am the one who has to find him?"

They both shrugged as if it was the most obvious thing in the world.

"You are the only one among us who *can* find him," Frank said and gave me his best puppy dog eyes.

"Okay..." I took in a deep breath, "Which is the last place you remember fighting with him?"

"I..." He thought for a solid minute, "....have no idea"

"Oh, come on!" I and Soovin exclaimed in unison.

"What?" He retorted back, "I am a human and humans make mistakes! I am sorry"

"Losing a human being is not a simple mistake! This is past apologies!" Soovin exclaimed.

"A human? You are an idiotic weasel and raccoon hybrid, that's what you are!" I shouted.

"Hey!" He protested, "Don't call Mom and Dad a weasel and a raccoon!"

I heard giggling and turned around.

There stood Anna, trying so hard to control her laughter that her face was red with the effort.

When we looked at her and rolled our eyes, she bursted into a fit of laughter, panting, "Wea...Weasel...Raccoon hybrid..."

An involuntary smile made its way to my lips.

Here we were in the middle of a crisis, and Anna was laughing as if it was the end of the world.

"Save some for tomorrow, will you?" I somewhat scolded her while smiling.

She just laughed harder in return until there were tears in her eyes.

"Really? Even 15-year-olds are laughing at me now!" Frank folded his arms and looked away like a five-year-old who had just been told that Santa wasn't real.

This made me and Soovin crack up as well and within a minute, we all were rolling on the floor, dying of laughter while Frank kept on shouting, "THAT'S ENOUGH! STOP

IT! I AM SERIOUS!"

It took all of us ten entire minutes to calm down and act more like CIA officers and an assassin and less like mentally ill lunatics.

Suddenly, Soovin froze.

For a moment, I thought he was trying to control his laughter but then, my eyes met his stony gaze. This was serious...in a *really* bad way.

I wasn't laughing anymore.

Soovin turned to Frank and asked in a panicked voice, "Where is that intruder who claimed to be a doctor?"

Frank leaned back proudly, "You see, this underappreciated, dashingly handsome, and criminally brave Officer has taken care of him"

"Frank, I am serious," Soovin got up, "Where is he?"

Frank looked at him dumbfounded, trying to process where Soovin was going with this and what had made him panic all of a sudden.

Anna, on the other hand, was way more intelligent and understood the concept of priorities.

She answered, "He is in the store room, tied to a chair with a gag in his mouth. He is unconscious possibly because one of you injected some anaesthesia into him"

Soovin cursed loudly.

"SOOVIN!" I protested, "Anna is here, will you *kindly* mind your *bloody language!?*"

"No, no, no, no..." He muttered with his eyes wide with anticipation and a hint of fear and regret in them which puzzled me.

"Soovin," I rushed to him as my heartbeat skyrocketed, "What is it?"

He met my gaze and shook his head slowly, "Han, I am sorry...I should've thought of this earlier...I...I am such an idiot!"

Frank's doorbell rang. Not once. Not twice. But in a rhythmic pattern as if a psychopath was at the door...a strangely familiar psychopath.

"Soovin, what's going on?" I asked him and immediately turned to Frank and demanded, "My gun"

Frank, who had finally caught on, rushed to the side table and took out my gun from one of its drawers. He threw it at me and I caught it just in time.

Meanwhile, Soovin kept on shaking his head and muttering how it was too late.

"Soovin, *what is going on?*" My tone wasn't very soft this time but was demanding answers urgently because just then, the sound of a door being broken echoed off the walls.

Then, the sound of multiple hurried footsteps met my ears.

Someone, no, *many* people were rushing overhead in Frank's house as if they were searching for something or...someone.

Soovin looked at me with a sorry look, "I...We screwed up, Han...big time"

CHAPTER SIX

A HEART-FELT SACRIFICE

"Will you tell us anything useful, Captain Obvious?" I huffed in irritation as the footsteps rushed over our heads.

There were A LOT of people.

"It's...him. It's GG," Soovin said as if he was doing a big reveal.

Frank turned to me, "Ya, he is not going to tell us anything useful, Han. Honestly, Soovin! How many psychopaths of that intellect have we dealt with? Of course, it's GG! Even Anna would know that"

"As a matter of fact, I did comprehend that before Dad's useful insights," Anna confirmed.

"That...I..." Soovin stammered in an effort to explain whatever was going on in his mind but failed miserably.

"The bookshelf does hide the entrance so-"

There was the sound of a door slamming and now, the men were directly above us.

Frank mouthed, 'It's not totally soundproof. Stay quiet'

All of us held our breaths. We were not scared of GG...well, not *that* much...but we didn't want him to find our secret base and ruin any chances of us staying in a safe haven while running from the CIA and him. We did NOT want that.

The muttering voices stopped out of the blue. I gulped as a bead of sweat trickled down my neck.

I mouthed, 'What made them freeze?'

All of them shrugged in response.

Then, a knock echoed in the silence.

I mentally cursed. He was using the sound to judge the presence of a secret room here. A familiar hysteric laughter marked his success and sent a shiver down my spine.

Any possibility of GG having a flicker of humanity faded from my mind.

"Aww...is someone there?" He mocked in his raspy voice, "Well since I can't find the entrance and no one is down there in danger of being shredded...Let's continue..."

All I could think was, *This is really bad,* before I heard the sound equivalent to at least 100 drills. Then, I heard the sound of concrete shattering or...shredding.

"He is a psycho!" I whisper-shouted.

"Now, who is Captain Obvious?" Soovin retorted for I wasn't the only one whose stress coping mechanisms were sass and humor.

I decided to ignore him, "We need a quick plan! Frank, exit route?"

"Behind that pillar," He whispered and advanced towards the said pillar.

Then, he stopped dead in his tracks and cursed.

"Anna is right here, Frank!" Soovin punched his arm.

Frank turned around, wide-eyed, and gulped, "The route will take us all out of here for sure but...its entrance can be covered only from the inside..."

"Someone has to stay here!?" Anna said horrified.

"What? No!" Frank exclaimed, "We just need to be fast on our feet so that they can't catch us...They will follow us but...We will make it!"

Frank's tone of voice was as uncertain as his comforting claim was false. We all knew we would never make it if that was the case.

If they had literally brought a mega drill with them, they were bound to be heavily armed and we would not stand a chance against god-knows-how many such men. Calling for a chase right now was like signing your own death warrant.

"Even if you morons have an exit route," GG shouted over the deafening sound of the drill, "You guys can't escape with an unconscious Hannah. So, it's better to give up. You never know! I might even show some mercy"

"He thinks I am still in a coma," I muttered under my breath as an idea sparked in my brain.

A rather dangerous yet genius idea.

"Quick! We can really use a head start right now. The ceiling is kind of thick. It will take them around five minutes to drill through it even with the monstrosity that's making that noise," Frank said.

I didn't hear a word of what he had said. I was busy working on my plan.

They would never agree to this, my mind pointed out, *But it is our best bet!*

I sighed. I had made my decision.

Frank hurried over to the pillar and placed his hand on one of the boxes of the peculiar design on the pillar. A green light greeted his hand and tested the handprint.

"Okay, that is pretty cool" Anna said in awe.

"Not bad, blondie," I acknowledged.

"Is that the highest praise I will ever get from you?" Frank rolled his eyes at me.

"Yup," I replied without any hesitation while my mind was busy screaming, *This might not work, Gorgin. And even if it does work, they are surely going to kill you after this.*

I know, I replied to my thoughts.

This tends to happen when you are jumping from one crisis to another. Walk half a mile in my shoes, and you are bound to lose some brain cells and start talking to yourself.

The pillar or the thing we all had assumed to be a pillar beeped and I heard metallic sounds from inside it. Now, I was *really* impressed but Frank did not need to know that.

The designed boxes on the pillar turned inwards and then, moved away together from the pillar, giving rise to a metallic ladder.

"Great design and all, Frank," I said, "But did your pea-sized brain think of reversing this transformation? Because if not, then, this is utterly useless, one use only-"

Suddenly, one of the boxes seeped inwards and a red button surfaced.

"You were saying?" Frank eyed me playfully but the environment turned grim shortly after when GG screamed in his psychotic way, "Here I come, my dear friends!"

"Anna, you first," I said and Anna obliged, "Then, Frank, and then, Soovin"

"And then you," Soovin added with a smile and my heart twisted in its cage.

Only if he knew...

I groaned in my head, *How is he making it this hard for me without even trying?*

"You good, Han?" He frowned, reading my face yet again.

"Yeah, what will happen to me?" I offered him a smile.

He raised his eyebrows. *How did this man see right through all my lies?*

"Han," He took a step toward me, "Are you-?"

"You guys can have all your sweet talk when we are safely out of here. Get a move on!" Frank said in a teasing voice.

He was halfway down the ladder and there was enough space for Soovin to start the descent.

Soovin smiled and shook his head at Frank. He looked at me with his emerald-green eyes that acquired a strange spark when he looked into my ocean-blue orbs. The spark hid so much affection.

He won't be able to take it again, Han, the sensible part of my brain seemed to say but I had made my decision.

He placed his warm hand on my cheek while staring at me with a tenderness that made my heart melt, "You really don't look very good, Han"

Meanwhile Frank muttered loud enough for us to hear, "Seriously, man? You have got to do that to my sister while I have a perfect view from here? It's a good thing, Anna is far ahead"

I could see Soovin smile and shake his head at Frank, "Your brother is *so* overprotective"

"Her *brother* can hear, you know?" Frank retorted.

I felt incredibly guilty, looking at them bickering that way. How could I take all of this away from them right after they had been devoid of any fun for a month...?

I kept on telling myself that I was *not* sacrificing myself. This plan had a chance to work...a 1% chance but a chance. I had completed missions with 0.1% chance of success, how hard could this be?

You know what you have to do, Officer, I told myself.

Soovin rolled his eyes at Frank and made his way toward the ladder.

I heard him whisper to Frank, "Thanks a lot for bursting my happy little bubble, Frank"

"Pardon me for pointing out that our doom is literally hanging over our heads, you infatuated idiot," He bit back.

They started descending.

Time was slowing down for me as I questioned and reevaluated my plan. I could feel a pit in my stomach.

My mind seemed to say, *Look at them. How can you do this to them?*

I swallowed all my paranoia, *It is for the best. You must do it for him, for them.*

I approached the ladder as well.

Soovin was waist down already. The ladder wasn't very long. Frank already had his one foot on the ground yet if Soovin was to step lower, he would hit his face.

"Soovin..." Tears choked my voice.

His neck snapped above. He took in my appearance as it dawned on him.

His eyes widened, "Han...I know what you are thinking, YOU CAN'T-"

"What the heck are you doing, Han?" Frank's panicked voice met my ears. He was catching up on the situation fast even from his limited view.

"I am sorry..." my voice trembled with the effort to stop my tears.

I could see tears in his eyes, "No, Han! I am not letting this happen again"

"HAN, YOU ARE COMING WITH US!" Frank screamed.

GG's sounds were getting nearer. They would be here within two minutes at maximum.

"I can't..." I said feebly.

"Han," a tear trickled down Soovin's face, "Please...Don't..."

I placed my trembling hand on his cheek as I failed to stop the strong flow of tears.

My voice sounded choked, "He thinks I am still in a coma. Soovin...I *had to* do this...It will buy you all some time..."

"I don't need time! I need you!" Soovin shouted through his tears.

Thankfully, the sound of the drill was deafening and GG wouldn't have heard it...He wouldn't know about them, he didn't need to.

I swallowed a fresh wave of tears, "I...Take care, Soovin...I am sorry"

Soovin shook his head and said in a heartbroken voice, "You can't do this to me...You...You can't leave me again, Han..."

"Get yourself together," I whispered through my own tears.

His voice was hoarse when he said, "Han...please"

I whispered with trembling lips, "I am sorry..."

Just like that, I pushed him away in a swift motion and jabbed the red button.

With that, Soovin disappeared from my view as GG's maniacal laughter seemed nearer than ever, "I will be there in barely a minute. You can run but you can't hide, fellows!"

CHAPTER SEVEN

ARE YOU FINE, GG?

I shook off all my emotions.

You don't have time, Gorgin, I reminded myself, *You better be quick.*

And quick I *was.*

Within barely a minute, I had dashed back to my bed, frantically connected some of the instruments to myself, and acted to be unconscious.

I could not rely on my vision for my eyes were closed. That meant I had to depend mainly on noise which was good but not good enough.

Still, I strained my ears to register every single sound and told my mind to work overtime for now if it wanted to live. I needed my ears to register even a pin drop because when GG is the one you are standing against, one can never be sure if the pin drop is from someone's hairpin or the safety pin of a hand grenade.

Suddenly, the voice of the drill doubled and then as abruptly, came to a halt.

They were here.

I kept on repeating in my mind, *Play dead. Play dead. Play dead. Don't move a single muscle. Don't flinch and don't even think about shivering.*

I heard a growl from the storeroom, where the fake doctor was lying unconscious according to Anna, "Make way for me"

This was followed by a lot of shuffling noises and my mind was trying its best to supply me a possible image of what was happening.

I almost peeked, *Are they really making human stairs for GG to descend or have I finally lost that last speck of sanity?*

Judging by the feeble and disguised grunts, I had not gone insane...yet.

I heard footsteps approach me and went completely still. It took a lot of effort to keep my breathing normal, in fact, steady and slower than normal so that the machines showed me in a coma.

"Hmm..." I felt a cold finger trace my jawline and then my chin, probably checking if I was wearing a face mask.

It took all my willpower not to flinch at that wrecked contact. Even the tip of his finger seemed to be frozen with hate and terror.

I almost sighed in relief when he lifted his finger off me, "Looks like they all have gone outside for a bit...leaving this precious gift here for me"

Heck no, I thought, *Go away, you son of a gun.*

"Where have they gone?" He rasped.

A panicked voice met my ears, "I-I don't k-know, Captain..."

"Are you afraid...?" GG's voice was inhumanely cold.

"N-n-Yes, Captain. I am sorry for this. It won't happen again," The desperation in the man's voice was evident enough to make even *me* have mercy on him even though he was my opponent in this face-off.

"Don't worry," GG's voice was psychotically calm, "Soovin was like my brother, his intellect almost matches mine. I didn't expect you to be successful at keeping an eye on him. He knows sneaking and weaselling around like the back of his hand. Oh, those were some good old days..."

Despite knowing that they were like brothers, hearing GG talk about Soovin that way made my skin crawl and gave me the urge to throw up. His nostalgic laughter didn't help my nausea either.

"T-thank you, Captain," I heard the man faintly whisper.

"Oh!" GG said in his typical psychotic way, "That doesn't mean I forgive you. You have made the same mistake twice. On top of that...You are *scared*. Now, *that* is something I can't let go easily-"

He shot his last shot, "It won't happen again, Captain!"

Stunned silence.

Silence that made me consider the idea of risking a peak to see what had happened to make all of the people go quiet.

GG growled in what I believed to be disbelief and utter shock, "You dared to interrupt me...?"

Judging by the sound of it, the guy was probably falling over GG's feet, begging for forgiveness.

I thought, *Such a shocked and mournful silence because he got interrupted? Man, what kind of psycho am I dealing with?*

Then, he showed me just what kind of psycho I was *actually* dealing with.

"You *are* scared, you *coward*," He spoke the word 'coward' as if he was spitting out poison, "Hmm...You all, what shall I do with someone who has made the same mistake twice, has dared to cut me off and over everything else is *scared?*"

"KILL HIM!" came the collective blood-thirsty chant of his men and women that made my jaw drop.

My mind went haywire, *KILL HIM FOR THAT?! THEY ALL ARE NUTS!*

A gunshot echoed in the room which made me shiver from head to toe.

I cursed in my mind, *COULDN'T YOU PLAY DEAD FOR LONGER, YOU IDIOT!?*

"Now...Would you look at that?" GG's playful voice pretty much announced that he had seen my stupid shiver, "Looks like someone is *not very* unconscious"

His voice was so close that I barely resisted another shiver, "Officer Gorgin, mind getting up?"

The heart monitor beeped. My heartbeat was increasing which just confirmed that I no longer was in a coma.

My mind frantically tried to weave an escape from this situation but couldn't find a solution.

Mr. Dune's voice rang in my ears, *If you don't see any escape route from a problem, make one. And if you can't make one...Perhaps it is not a problem after all.*

I asked my mind, *Is it really a problem?*

You bet it is, it replied.

So much for a philosophical advice that claimed to save lives, I thought bitterly, *Think, Gorgin...*

Then, I once again pursued a rather dumb idea that somehow seemed to work for me.

Don't ask me how because I have no idea.

I let my heartbeat increase which was not hard since I *was* panicking. Then, I started panting a bit, my eyes still clenched shut. I gripped the bed sheets tighter than ever. Imagining it to be GG's neck made it a lot easier.

I abruptly tore off my oxygen mask just like I had done earlier. I surely deserve an Oscar for the act I put up for him. An act that *GG bought.*

"She is regaining consciousness..." I heard him mutter in a serious tone.

I felt like jumping in joy, *This buffoon is actually falling for it!*

"I-I...GET A DOCTOR!" I couldn't believe what I was hearing.

GG. Gruesome Ghoul was *panicking* that too to *save* a life, *my life.* At that point, I was pretty sure I was dreaming all of it. Maybe I had slipped into a coma again? Because *this* cannot be happening.

His voice offered a peek at some underlying emotions that did not suit him at all. He was a cold-hearted sociopath...but then, why was he panicking...?

"Captain, we don't have a doctor to come on a quick notice-"

"GET KAVIN! HE IS IN THE STORE ROOM. WAKE THAT BASTARD UP!?"

I continued my act as I grew more and more puzzled by every passing second.

WHY WAS HE SO FRANTIC TO SAVE ME? HE HAD *LITERALLY* ATTEMPTED TO SLICE MY THROAT WITHOUT A THOUGHT EARLIER!

After barely three seconds, a woman reported, "He is strongly out, Captain. Waking him up would take at least half an hour"

"GET A PARAMEDIC WITHIN SECONDS, I DON'T CARE!?"

Now, I was starting to freak out.

GG showing emotions was a strange and creepy sight that flooded my mind with a billion questions most of them were along the lines of, *WHY ON EARTH IS HE ACTING THIS WAY?!*

A new voice came, "Captain, I have some medical training and a little experience with coma patients. I think I can-"

A ruffling noise was heard as if GG was grabbing the man by his collar.

GG said in a grave voice, "I don't care what you do. I want her alive. I want Sharlet-"

GG froze for a bit but gathered himself quickly, "Officer Gorgin is an important bait for my plans. Don't mess this up, young one"

I made a mental note to ask Soovin about a *Sharlet*.

"I would give it my absolute best, Captain," The man replied with confidence.

"*Best* is not enough," He hissed, overcome by rage, "If she dies, so do you"

The man's confidence was admirable, "Don't worry, Captain. It won't come to that. I won't let you down"

At that point, I was getting kind of sick of panting like a dog for so long.

After studying the machines for a bit, the man reported, "She is stable, Captain"

I took that as my cue to slowly normalize my breathing. I had no words to express how much gratitude I felt for that guy for relieving me of the misery of panting any further. My lungs were starting to hurt. I didn't even know that was possible, but here I was, finding things out the hard way as usual.

He continued, "It is natural for the breathing to be laboured when one wakes up from a coma but..."

"But what?" GG snapped.

He continued a bit hesitantly, "I am not sure about this yet, Captain but...I doubt that the gunshot could be a trigger strong enough to wake her up from a coma..."

All my feelings of gratitude towards the guy vanished into thin air and I wanted to kick him between the legs.

Some part of my brain went, *Well, attacking anyone on sight is pretty natural for patients waking up from a coma...Since luck is on your side for now, you might give that a shot as well...*

"Are you implying that she is faking...?" GG asked and I began reconsidering the option to get up and take my chances against all the heavily armed people in a shootout.

"Well...There could be a lot of reasons for that. I am not experienced enough to judge that but it could be one possibility...out of a hundred"

GG seemed to be deep in thought for he didn't say anything for a solid minute which wasn't helping my anxiety.

He finally spoke, "Well...In that case-"

"I am sorry for interrupting, Captain but it is an emergency, level 7"

"What is it?" I could hear the anticipation in his voice.

The fact that he had shot a man for interrupting him and he was not even mad at this man for doing the same gave me a feeling that a level 7 emergency was bad...really bad...but for me or for them, I couldn't tell.

"Soovin is rushing towards us while a CIA Officer, Frank Gorgin along with a teenage girl is desperately trying to stop his vehicle"

I wanted to facepalm so bad.

Soovin. Of course, that emotional idiot would come back and try to save me after I forcefully pushed him away.

I had no idea whether to be mad at him or hug him at sight.

Now, I don't know what I expected GG to do. I knew he was not going to just leave me here and get scared of Soovin but I certainly did not expect him to do what he did next.

"I am not taking any chances...She can handle some light anaesthesia, right?"

"I am not sure about that, Captain. I don't have much experience or knowledge to judge it"

GG cursed under his breath, "Screw it...Tell the pilot to bring the helicopter down. We are going back to the base...Settle her in my helicopter, NOW"

I gulped, *Maybe faking a coma wasn't a good idea, after all...*

CHAPTER EIGHT

GG Tries Skydiving

You need to escape, I thought as a sick cult of psychopaths carried me to a helicopter to take me to their base.

Man, life really had gone downhill.

I could now half-open my eyes because GG believed that to be natural for patients waking up from a coma.

I could watch clearly just how big of a lunatic I was dealing with. Oh, lucky me.

GG stepped inside and sat next to me, smirking, "Poor Officer Gorgin, look at you. Can't move a finger or your foul mouth, only your eyes. What a shame..."

"I will bite your head off with this very mouth," I hissed. I was getting pretty agitated with him.

He raised his eyebrows, "Well...Officer, seems like you are slowly regaining your senses"

"And you are losing yours," I bit back, "Wait, my bad! You don't have any to begin with, knucklehead!"

I could see two of his men trying to hold their laughter and shock. Given that GG's face was getting purple with rage, they were doing a pretty terrible job at it.

His kingdom was built upon mainly fear. Disrespecting him in front of his people was like chipping away at one of the concrete pillars of his empire and I was more than happy to do the job.

"Control your tongue, Officer," He growled, "Or I will-"

"What? Kill me?" I rolled my eyes as I gave the impression that my entire body was paralyzed except my mouth and face, "I am the bait, remember? You need me alive, you dumb rock"

"Oh really? I can-Wait, you were conscious when I said that?"

I continued my plan of getting on his nerves until he did a mistake in frustration, "How else will I know what you said, you dumbo dumb dumb? In case you didn't know, coma patients can hear at times"

I spewed some more random facts about coma to keep him occupied while I thought of some more enraging insults and a plan to get me out of this maniac's helicopter.

"Mind your tongue, Officer or I will-"

"Cut it out? Wow, how very original of you! Really? That's the best you can do?"

"MIND IT!" GG got up and hovered over me threateningly, "Soovin wouldn't know that his dear daughter's mother is missing a tongue before an exchange is made successfully"

My heart was beating out of my chest yet I put on a bored face, stuck out my tongue, and mocked him, "Go ahead then, Mr. Tongue cutter. You cut my tongue out and my brother Frank, Soovin, and I will cut you-"

"DON'T PLAY WITH FIRE, OFFICER!?"

"Fire? You are being extremely generous to yourself. You are more like a spark generated by an out-of-fuel lighter"

That was it. One of his men cracked up and GG saw his not-so-hidden grin.

"Funny, is it?" He growled.

Everyone on the helicopter froze and it felt like the air itself was holding its breath for what was about to happen.

In a swift motion, he grabbed the man by the collar, smashed open the helicopter's door, and threw him off the helicopter causing the other men to shiver with fright. A shrill scream was heard and that was it.

A life taken without any hesitation or remorse.

My skin tinged with terror but still, I put on a face, recalled my CIA training, and said, "Well, that's a bummer"

"Careful, Officer," GG lunged towards me and stopped a centimetre away from me, "The next one could be you. Then, Soovin and your dear brother would be way too heartbroken to get up and face me. Trust me, it won't be a problem"

"You will really kill me?"

He smirked menacingly, "Keep your tongue out of control and I just might. We both know I will"

"Woooh, hurray! Do it, please"

GG did a double-take. He was not used to such responses.

He was too shocked to reply at first, "I beg your pardon...?"

"Do it...pretty please? I am sick of my life anyway! All I do is try to stay alive and run from one place to another. Plus, how painful can it really be?"

At that point, I myself had no idea what I was saying. It's safe to say that all these problems I was stuck in were finally getting to my mental health and boy could that land me in some serious trouble with a sociopath?

GG threw his hands in the air and screamed like a kid throwing a tantrum, "What on earth is wrong with these people!?"

"Is that a yes...?"

Acting foolish wasn't a piece of cake but man, was I owning it at that moment?

GG muttered defeatedly under his breath, "I know waking up from coma can mess up a person's mental state but never had I imagined a case could be this bad! It's more dizzy and dreamy than foolish and irritating"

I saw my chance, *He thinks I am in a dreamy state...Perfect.*

A plan formed in my mind but for it to work, I had to act even more stupid and immature, if such a level of stupidity existed. Guess, I was about to find out.

I focused, *What is one embarrassing thing that I would rather die than do right now? That ought to convince him fully that I am in a dreamy state and not myself.*

A horribly embarrassing scenario crept into my mind.

I almost screamed, *NO! I AM NOT DOING THAT!*

My conscience replied, *A bit of embarrassment or your prime duty, Officer? Choose wisely.*

I took in a deep breath, *I can't believe I am really doing this.*

"Hey, Gavin," I called him casually as if he were an old friend of mine and not a literal maniac kidnapper.

He flinched at the mention of his real name and scowled but I cut him off, "Will you tell me something?"

"I am not bound to answer your questions, especially when you are technically high, Officer. Stay put or I might lose my calm. I am pretty short-tempered as you should know after I taught you a lesson by using your Mom"

He had stepped on a major nerve.

It really was a miracle that I didn't tear him apart with my bare hands.

I recalled Mr. Dune's advice, *Anger is your biggest enemy, Office Gorgin. It makes one lose control and that's something you don't want on a mission. Swallow your anger instead of wasting your energy on violence, let your victory in the final battle speak for itself.*

Keep the act up, I told myself, *You can kill him in peace later.*

I smiled goofily to hide the bloodlust in my eyes, "Tell me about Soovin"

He did a double take again and then smirked evilly, "His backstory? That weak coward couldn't tell you himself, could he? I would be obliged to do the honours, Officer. The *innocent Soovin* is a cold-blooded killer-"

"No," I waved my hand dismissingly and acted as if I was slowly getting dizzy, "I meant his likes and dislikes. Was he always so oblivious or did meeting me changed him?"

Even hearing myself say that, I wanted GG to throw me out of there. That seemed like a way better option. I had begun questioning my plan's rationality.

My second thoughts were overwhelming, *Is it really worth it?*

Meanwhile, GG was speechless. He had not seen *that* coming and catching him off guard was all I needed.

I flipped and kicked him in the face with my 'paralyzed' body. The shock had dimmed his and his people's reflexes. The element of surprise gave me an advantage over their heavy armoury but it wouldn't stay like that for long.

I needed to be quick.

GG's reflexes were swift but shock was dulling them while anger acted as a catalyst for mine.

He fumbled and gathered himself as his half-dazed men finally reached for their guns.

I love this pressure point, I thought as I swiftly gave all of them a taste of death touch.

GG lunged at me barehanded for the kick had already made his gun fall out of the helicopter. I was expecting it and swiftly step-sided.

I grabbed him by the neck and pushed him towards the door of the helicopter that he himself had opened to throw one of his men out. He was not expecting *that* either and I cherished the priceless look on his face when he realized that the tables had turned.

He held on to the edge of the helicopter's open door firmly with his well-toned arm while I threw the rest of his body outside.

I reached to the pilot and whispered, "Get up, your whirlybird has been hijacked"

I knocked him out cold and put the chopper on auto-pilot.

Meanwhile, GG was pretty busy. With his free hand, he hastily took out a handheld transceiver and spoke into it, "CODE 101-"

I snatched it from his grip. He could do little to stop me while dangling 10, 000 feet in the air.

I spoke into it, "The code is that you little pups need to back the heck up. If any helicopter is within three feet of us, your dear Boss is going to go skydiving with no safety on"

Four out of the five helicopters backed away immediately. I squinted and shook my head on seeing the last helicopter readying a machine gun.

I rolled my eyes, "Setting a machine gun might cause all you pets to become stray dogs. Watch it, you half-witted wretches"

GG was trying to signal something but dangling out of a helicopter didn't make it easy to communicate in sign language.

I turned to him, "That includes you, Mister. You are not the sharpest tool in the shed, are you?"

He just growled and then, made the universal gesture of retreat.

I smirked, "That's right, knuckleheads. Back the heck up before I lose my patience and he his grip on life"

Although somewhat reluctantly, the last helicopter backed up, making me smile in triumph.

I turned to GG once again, "Looks like it's you versus me again"

"YOU WILL PAY FOR THIS!" He roared over the wind.

His face was getting pale with the effort of holding himself up.

I clicked my tongue mockingly, "Getting weak, are you? Want this 'bait' to help you relieve the pain you are in?"

His eyes widened and I could see the panic he was trying to hide.

It was the best and most satisfactory thing I had seen in my entire life, "You would not do that. You *cannot* do that"

I shrugged, "Oh, given the hell you have made me go through, I just might"

I leaned close to him and whispered with flames of revenge in my eyes, "This is for my mom"

With that, I kicked him on the face as he went down screaming, enjoying some dangerous skydiving.

CHAPTER NINE

A NOT-SO-PRETTY HELICOPTER

I stomped my foot and cursed loudly as I saw one of the helicopters rush to save GG and succeed.

"OH COME ON!?" I screamed, "If I was the one falling, there would have been no chance of survival. Why is life *so* unfair?"

I continued my complaints as I took control of the helicopter.

I couldn't help but admire the helicopter's build. The controls were as smooth as butter. The obedient little chopper seemed to change its path even at the slightest of indication and I was in love with its control panel.

"I am not returning this little boy to him anytime soon," I muttered as I flew a safe distance away from the five helicopters to contemplate my next move.

"How can I contact them...?" I wondered aloud. Soovin had probably gone crazy when he found me missing and Frank and Anna were probably pulling their hair out because of him.

I was deep in thought as I was miles ahead of the other helicopters who were probably way too busy saving their

Boss to see my direction of departure, "Where could they be...?"

I had no idea. Only they knew the answer.

My mind's gears turned, *So, why not ask them?*

I glanced at the unconscious pilot and searched him for a phone.

"GG has probably installed the tech needed to attend a phone call while the craft is airborne," I muttered to reassure myself.

I used the pilot's fingerprint to unlock his phone and found Soovin's number already saved on it as 'Boss no. 2'.

It took quite some effort to shake my uneasiness off.

He did work with them earlier as another Boss, I thought and pressed the call button.

The phone was picked on the first ring itself and I immediately learned a lesson to always keep the phone a safe distance away from your ears for the sake of your eardrums.

Soovin's voice warmly greeted me at some hundred decibels, "GAVIN, I SWEAR TO GOD, IF THERE IS A SINGLE SCRATCH ON HER, I WILL CHOP YOU INTO A TRILLION FREAKING PIECES AND-"

I tried to mask my smile and cut him off in a robotic voice, "The person you are trying to reach is currently busy having a brief appointment with Satan. You can either wait or talk to me instead because he won't be taking calls anytime soon"

"HAN!" I could hear the relief in his voice, "It's not funny! Where the heck are you? Are you fine? What happened? *Why on earth* did you do that back at Frank's house? Have you lost your mind-"

"Woah, there," I cut him off, "Put the general talk on hold right now. I am in GG's helicopter and I am pretty sure he would have some kind of locator installed in it. We don't have much time. So, spill your location quickly. I will come there with this heavenly beauty"

There was a short silence on the other end and then, came Frank's voice, " (11, 3) (10, 4) (2, 4) (7, 3) (6, 4) (5, 3) (10, 3) (8, 3) (7, 5) (4, 4)"

"Hang on, blondie," I said and grabbed a stray piece of paper and pen lying near the unconscious pilot, "You are going to have to repeat that. Not gonna lie, you sure are getting experienced in this stuff"

"Oh, you bet," He repeated the sequence.

I deciphered, 'PLAYGROUND'

"Big or small?" I asked, not stating the exact location just in case if GG had a hidden voice recorder installed in the helicopter.

"The most used one," He replied crisply.

He sighed as he seemed to lower his guard, "So, it's really you and not some imposter, ha? You have got a lot of explanation to do when you come by, might I add"

I groaned, "I do, don't I?"

"Yes, you do," came Anna's voice, "And you better be quick"

"I am on my way, princess," I replied as I increased the speed of the helicopter, "Damn, this thing sure is fast"

"Careful," Soovin said, "No more stunts or I will do something"

"Like what?" I chuckled.

"Oh trust me, you don't want to know," He said in a threatening tone which highlighted how serious he was.

I gulped at his tone, "Jeez! Fine, no need to throw threats. I have heard enough of them in the past hour to last a lifetime"

"He threatened you?" His voice became serious, "Han, what did that loggerhead say to you?"

"Quite a lot of stuff actually...like cutting my tongue out for starters," I smirked even though he couldn't see it.

"Then, what did you do?"

I grinned, "I gave him a black eye, I believe...and oh, I also threw him out from 10, 000 feet in the air"

"That's my girl!" I could hear his chuckle which was followed by two very familiar coughs.

I rolled my eyes while checking my position, "I'll be there within ten minutes. Meanwhile, buy those two idiots some cough drops if you please"

Frank's playful and mocking voice made crimson color spread in my cheeks, "Oh, I believe we are just fine"

"Jokes aside," Soovin said, "Han, be careful"

"Okay, *Mom,*" I shook my head at him, "See you within ten minutes"

I cut the call and turned my helicopter a few degrees south...little did I know my life was about to go just the same way.

I was seven minutes in on my short journey and I was already hovering over the playground Frank had mentioned, the one where we used to play the most.

I slowly landed the helicopter and I could already see my three favourite people in the entire world rushing towards me.

I got out of the helicopter and was engulfed by the trio.

"Really?" I laughed, "I was barely gone for a few hours!"

"Well, you gave the impression of a lot longer than that," Anna grumbled.

We all separated from the group hug and Soovin immediately shot daggers at me.

He said exasperatedly, "You are very fond of risking your life even when not needed, aren't you?"

"Well, I am not the only one!" I retorted, "You fancy running right into the mouth of danger, don't you? You *had* to rush back when you three barely escaped that too when you *knew* there were more than a dozen heavily armed people!"

"Well, did you expect me to let GG do whatever he wanted with you?!"

"I am not a kid!?"

"You sure are acting like one!"

"And you are not-?"

"STOP IT BOTH OF YOU!?" Frank screamed, "You guys are worse than bickering teenagers!"

"As a teenager, I can confirm," Anna added.

"Whatever," I muttered, "How did they even get to us?"

Soovin shifted uneasily and unconsciously rubbed his forearm where his tattoo was.

"Soovin," I asked a bit softly, "How did they get to us?"

"Well..." He sighed, "You know, the thing is these are not just some fancy tattoos for aesthetic purposes"

"And?" Frank prompted.

"They...GG has...transplanted little trackers inside his men. These tattoos just mark the existence of such trackers"

I diverted my gaze to his forearm and then, to his eyes. My question was clear - 'Do you have that tracker inside you as well?'

He replied, "He has that tracker installed in only the men who work *under* him"

Not beside him, He didn't say it out loud but he didn't need to. It was pretty obvious...for me at least.

"What do you mean by that?" Anna raised her eyebrows.

"Nothing," we both replied at the same time earning another raise of eyebrows.

"Doesn't look like it," She argued.

"You are banging your head on a wall, Anna," Frank said with a secretive wink and she grinned.

"I don't appreciate you having inside jokes with Anna," I told him, "Your mind isn't very holy"

He decided to change the topic and patted the helicopter, "Had a good ride in this little guy?"

"Oh, you bet. This is a work of art. The controls? Smooth as butter," I frowned, "It was almost... *suspiciously* easy..."

"You spoke too soon, Officer," GG's voice sent a shiver down my spine.

I turned so fast towards the helicopter that my head got a little hazy.

His voice boomed nonetheless, "Haven't forgotten our little tattoos, have you, bro?"

Soovin froze.

Frank stood in front of Anna protectively and I reflexively loaded my gun.

"I see you had my little helicopter all for yourself, Officer. And you enjoyed it! You know what? I'll give it to you right now...as a gift of course"

"Back away," I told Frank while I grabbed Soovin.

I don't like the sound of that, I thought.

But it was too late.

GG spoke loud and clear, "CHOPPER F-2, ISSUE SELF-DESTRUCT"

I pushed Soovin away from the wrecked helicopter which didn't look as pretty now and thought, *Oops! A bit late to escape myself now.*

But Soovin turned and grabbed me before leaping away from the chopper, taking me with him.

Great job, Soovin, I thought as time slowed down for me,
Now it's a bit late for both of us.
      Just like that the world went black for me...

65

CHAPTER TEN

BETRAYAL STINGS

I woke up in a hospital...a rather ancient hospital whose ceiling was blacker than my future.

My first thought was, *I am getting sick of being hospitalized. Stop for god's sake!*

The second one was, *Why am I here?*

I strained my mind and recalled the blast.

Panic rose inside my chest, *Where are the others? Who admitted me here?*

I sat a bit upright and my lingering gaze landed on Soovin's limp figure lying on the bed next to mine.

I called him uncertainly, "Soovin...?"

He flinched in response but that was it.

Suddenly, I heard a surprised voice, "Han, you are awake!"

I muttered, "I am getting sick of waking up in hospital beds right now"

"Well, then, don't do things that land you here!" He sat on the edge of my bed.

"Oh, my bad! Because *I* was the one who invited GG to blast the helicopter, wasn't I?" I rolled my eyes at him and then, a sudden thought made me frown.

"Frank, where is Anna?" I asked.

He shifted uncomfortably, "Han...she..."

"SHE WHAT?" I didn't bother controlling my voice which was matching my heart rate as my mind supplied me with the worst-case scenarios.

"Woah, CHILL, okay?" Frank held up his hands, "She has just gone to the restroom!"

I punched him in the face, not bothering to be gentle, "That is *not* something to joke about, you little weasel!"

He groaned, clutching at his nose, "Sorry, okay? I do stupid stuff when I am under stress, you know that!"

I let out a sigh and resisted the urge to smack him again, "You good?"

"I wasn't the one right next to the blast," He shrugged.

"You brought us *here?*" My CIA side started to take control, "This is a *hospital*, Frank. We are foolishly exposed!"

"This is an *ancient* hospital with barely any facilities apart from the basic ones, definitely not enough tech to create a problem for us. Plus, it was pretty close and you both were unconscious after the helicopter exploded. I and Anna were pretty frenzied"

I glanced toward Soovin, "How is he?"

He shrugged, "The doctor said that his condition was the same as yours. You have woken up. So, he should be awake soon"

My stomach grumbled, "Man, I am starving. Do you have something?"

He picked up the bag sitting on the small table beside my bed and opened it. He offered me a burger saying, "Soovin had already bought these for all of us before..."

"The helicopter went up in flames?" I supplied.

"Yeah...Anyway, you enjoy your meal. I am going to go and check on Anna"

With that, he left the room as I devoured my burger.

The burger was appetizing but I couldn't enjoy it for my mind was somewhere else.

GG had almost killed all of us with a simple command.

That was not a child's play. Who knew what he could do if he got a proper chance? He must not be happy about what happened or what *I did* to him in the helicopter. He was probably fuming with rage. In that state, he could do a lot of *inhumane* things that we would not like.

My mind drifted as I recalled something.

Sharlet. Who was she?

GG had mentioned her unintentionally and when he had mentioned her, he seemed so...bare as if he-

"Lost in thought, Officer?" An awfully familiar voice brought me back to reality.

I gulped, *Wait, it can't be-It is surely not him; I must be going bonkers-*

"I warned you not to play with fire, didn't I?" GG rasped and I turned around with a jolt.

Adrenaline surged through my body on seeing his hungry and evil look. He was here...with two dozen heavily armed men this time.

He snapped his fingers and his people locked the door.

I thought miserably, *Is this really how I die...?*

"Why are you here?" I held my ground although my heart was beating out of my chest.

"Who is not the sharpest tool in the shed, now, ha?" He laughed, "I am here to finish the task I was doing, of course"

"What makes you think you will succeed this time?" I smirked confidently as if I was not a second away from being killed.

"I love your attitude!" He smiled like a true sociopath, "What a shame it is about to be broken rather brutally"

He clicked his tongue playfully and took his seat while toying with his gun.

I instinctively reached for mine but when all 24 barrels of guns were pointed at me in a flip second, I decided to drop the idea.

Great, I thought, *so no gun...Perfect, just perfect...*

"Aww..." He leaned back in his chair, "You want your gun? Feeling vulnerable and empty-handed without it?"

"No, because soon my hands would be pretty full carrying your severed head," I bit back as I mentally weighed my options.

"Oh, I am not going to make the same mistake again. You can bet on it, Officer. I am a light-headed guy, you see"

Part of me was tempted to yell 'Sharlet' and see just how light-headed he was but I decided to save my masterstroke for later and snorted instead.

GG smirked, "Show all the sass you want to because soon, you are going to be way too broken to even utter a joke or smile"

"For sure..." I muttered loud enough for him to hear.

He just looked at me and smiled.

His smile was freaking me out...he had something...*a really bad* something that he was pretty confident about.

"Now, you have two options," GG leaned forward, "Go with us peacefully and cherish our hospitality as our dear guest-"

"Hell, no. The second one, please," I straightened a bit, ready to spring up at any moment.

"Or..." He smirked more evilly than ever, "Soovin dies"

My heart missed a beat and my eyes immediately darted towards him.

"Oh, no need to worry about your old friend. I won't let that happen," I replied, getting up confidently and calmly as if I couldn't feel the bile in my mouth.

He smiled wider than ever, "Is that so...?"

I could feel a pit in my stomach but I held our eye contact and rolled my shoulders, signalling that I was ready to tear my way out through his men.

He clapped once and all his men formed a ring around Soovin...looking so mad and dangerous that I had the urge to hide in my hospital blanket until all of them magically disappeared.

"You see...I might have partly forgiven him for what he did but..." GG gestured towards his bloodthirsty pack of dogs, "They haven't. All of them are itching for some revenge, and believe me when I say," he leaned forward and whispered menacingly, "They will tear him apart with their bare hands"

All of them banged their guns to show their readiness and all I could wonder was, *HOW THE HELL IS HE SLEEPING THROUGH ALL THIS? I AM GOING TO KILL HIM!?*

Thinking that waiting for Frank to help me was my only option, I said, "You know, Gav-"

He flicked his fingers and a knife was jabbed into Soovin's pillow, half a centimetre beside his Adam's apple.

I froze on the spot.

"Careful, Officer," He rasped, "I am the one in control right now"

I shook my head as I felt a bit dizzy for some reason but continued, "You are missing one thing"

"Frank can bang this door all he wants, my men will hold it together till their last breath," He winked, "*And* Soovin is not going to get up anytime soon, I assure you that...Seems like it's you versus me *yet again*, Officer"

"Well, in that case," I took out my gun and he gestured his men to stay there until the next order, "I plan to go down fighting"

I lunged at him but he had indeed learned from his mistake and was incredibly quick on his feet...or was I slowing down...?

I tried to kick him but he sidestepped easily and I almost lost my balance.

I thought, *What is going on? Something is not right.*

"A little rusty, are you?" He growled before slamming my head into the cabinet dedicated to medical supplies.

For whatever reason he was anxious to save my life back there, it was no longer the case. He knew that a head injury could induce coma again but he didn't bother to hesitate a single bit. He was not going to go easy on me this time.

I thought bitterly, *How do I keep on getting so lucky back-to-back?*

I tried to shake the dizziness away but the world around me seemed to be floating.

"Oh little delicate fellow, feeling dizzy?" Even GG's voice seemed somewhat distant.

He grabbed my elbow and I failed to shake even his weak grip off.

How was I suddenly this weak?

My eyes widened in realization.

I murmured unintelligently, "The burger...Soovin..."

"Aww...He brought that for you, didn't he?" He mocked.

My mind was swimming as I tried to process everything, "How...Soovin...Frank..."

GG chuckled and muttered, "You forgot, didn't you, Officer? An assassin is a crook by all standards and..." He leaned closer for me to hear his emphasized words, *"Must not be trusted"*

I had almost lost my vision yet, I could still hear Mr. Dune in the back of my mind, *Each betrayal begins with trust, Officer. You need to be very careful about who you decide to trust.*

Then, the world melted away for me as a sense of betrayal pierced my heart.

All I could think before collapsing to the ground was, *Soovin...How could you...?*

CHAPTER ELEVEN

GG's MASTERPLAN

I woke up gradually. I didn't have a nightmare but that was not an issue because my life itself had become one.

Although I was awake, I did not open my eyes for I was being haunted by memories. My thoughts were too loud on their own and absorbing the details of my surroundings was impossible with a debate going on in my head along with me being tormented by memories.

Frank saying, *Soovin had already bought these for all of us...*

GG saying, *He bought that for you, didn't he?*

That horrible smile of his revolved in front of my eyes as by ears rung...*An assassin is a crook by all standards and must not be trusted.*

I felt broken, *I was ready to go down fighting for him for his protection, and he...*

I shook myself awake, *You don't have any proof and you can't possibly take GG's word for it...but Frank said Soovin had bought the burger...And who says no one on Earth can fool him? He must have missed a tiny detail or something!*

Even when I thought so, I felt empty and scarred.

Despite knowing that Soovin paid extra attention to details and it was next to impossible for him to miss out on adulteration with food he had bought, I tried my best to defend him. Still, no matter what, the fact remained - He had bought me the burger that was responsible for knocking me out mid-fight.

I took a deep breath.

In any other scenario, I could have thought of a trillion possible explanations of how Soovin was innocent and a billion theories of what could have possibly happened. Then, I would have slowly eliminated them one by one until I had a handful of contrasting yet potential theories.

However, this was not the case this time. I was emotionally hurt and that was clouding my sense of judgement.

On one hand, I couldn't believe Soovin would do something like that but on the other, my paranoia was screaming, *Every single thing you touch turns to ashes anyways!*

In short, my mind was a horrible place to be in at that moment.

I couldn't take it anymore. So, I decided to open my eyes and allowed my cold-hearted professional side to take over because...my other side was already shattered into a million pieces and ineligible to do anything but pine till I die.

Get in the zone, Officer Gorgin, I thought and swallowed all my emotions.

I will have a lot of time to weep once I escape from wherever I was.

I finally opened my eyes.

I was lying on the cold, black-tiled floor of a room.

I almost sighed in relief, *As long as it's not another hospital bed, it's fine, I'll take it!*

The room was dimly lit. It was less of a room and more of a prison cell with the bars missing. My eyes immediately darted to the 'hidden' button camera on the wall, camouflaged inside a clock.

Smart, I almost said aloud.

There was a single bed and a table and chair. Upon the table, lay a note.

I advanced towards it and unfolded it, 'If you are awake, I'll be with you shortly. Make yourself at home, Officer. You'll be here for a while'

"GG," I hissed with a mixture of disgust and fury.

Just then, the door swung open, making me roll my eyes and mutter, "Speak of the devil and he doth appear"

"Fancy your new room?" GG asked with a smile as his men closed the door firmly behind him.

I bit my tongue as I had the impulse to give him a reply that would have had my mom wash my mouth with soap.

He sat on the chair and said, "Feeling better, Officer? You have been unconscious for quite a while"

"What do you want?" I kept my tone crisp.

He chuckled, "Straight to business, are we?"

I gave him a death glare which only made him laugh more heartily.

"Fine," He held up his hands, "Here is the deal, Officer"

I leaned forward, finally interested in the conversation.

"You have to die"

I gave him a blank stare and then, rolled my eyes, "Really? We both know that if you wanted me to die, you would have killed me while I was unconscious"

"I would've...but that's for *cowards,*" He said.

"That is exactly why I anticipated it from you," I bit back.

I noticed his demeanour change as he leaned forward and gritted out with a clenched jaw, "I am not a *coward*"

I had a billion nasty and sassy replies ready but something about his present mental state made me hesitate. The way his eyes had turned dark as if he was somewhere else.

"Why do you say *coward* as if it is an insult?" I asked, delicately tapping into his mental state.

Every criminal had a back story. Work in the CIA for seven years and you will be well aware of the fact that, *Evil is not born, it is made.*

I had to know what had made him this way, partly out of curiosity and partly because it was important for me to understand who I was dealing with. However, I didn't plan on forgiving or improving him *at all* because *Evil is not born, it is a choice.*

I just wanted to safeguard myself by identifying and avoiding pressing his triggers because despite if he was a victim or villain, he was a straight-up psycho and I was not mentally ill enough to do anything for him except kill him.

GG was lost in thought as if I had stepped on a trigger. Then, he shuddered and quickly gathered himself yet again.

He looked at me with cold contempt, "Officer, don't try to get in my head because trust me, you are not ready to see the demons inside me"

"You drop the game, and so will I!" I shrugged.

"You *really* want to know about my plans, ha?" His eyes showcased how psychic he was getting, "I will tell you if you want but remember, Officer, *Curiosity killed the cat*"

"*But satisfaction brought it back,* Use the entire proverb or not at all, you Lamebrain"

"Well, then," He carelessly leaned back in his chair as if he was just recounting his tasks for the day, "I am using you as bait to lure my old buddy, Soovin, your brother, and that little demon, of course. He has something with him that interests me or rather, something *mine* that he forgot to return before going rogue. I was going to make this very offer with him back when I had your mom and his lovely daughter but you sneaked out that demon and I knew Soovin *would* come for your mom but he will not hand me back what he took all those years ago. This thing is important, you see"

"More important than an innocent life?" I asked in disbelief.

His look turned grim, "More important than a billion innocent lives...Anyways! I had thought that since you all seemed to be getting pretty close with each other, kidnapping you would surely force him to come back here and return me what's mine. However, believe it or not, even I did not anticipate that he would double-cross you"

I flinched at his sore reminder that felt like a painful poke to my heart but regained my composure. This was important.

He laughed hysterically, "I can't believe I actually thought that *he,* of all people, had changed for the better. Oh, how stupid I feel for believing that horrible cooked-up lie!"

My mind was working overtime, *His body posture suggests that he is telling the truth but why would Soovin...It's GG, Gorgin, he would surely know how to amend his body posture to make you believe him. Leave the theories for later, just absorb the facts to draw possible conclusions.*

He continued, "Now that I know that he is still his old self and doesn't give a damn about you"

I almost snapped his neck in half...almost.

"My plan seemed doomed but I am a damn adjustable man! He might not care about you but I know for sure he has a sweet spot for that little demon he left everything for-

"

"Her name is Anna, you know," I was getting sick of him calling that beautiful princess a demon for the fourth time.

He waved his hand dismissively at me, "So, I will exchange you for her in the first place, and then, I will use her as a bait to reclaim what's mine"

I scoffed, "No matter if he *double-crossed me,* as you claim he did, or even if there is something else going on, he would *never* send Anna to you for me. Mister moron of a mastermind, your entire plan is doomed, just like your future"

I let a laugh slip out but my skin tingled when I saw his evil smirk, "Oh, Officer...You got that part wrong. I don't need *him* to make the exchange for I already know he won't. You see, that little demon loves you way too much and..."

A horrible yet insanely possible scenario crept into my mind as my heartbeat fastened with anticipation. I gulped.

I asked despite half knowing the answer, "And what...?"

His smirk widened as he said, "I might take a bit of advantage of that"

"She would never," My claim sounded wild even to me.

"Aww, Officer," He laughed, "We both know she will..."

My mind was working at lightning speed. His plan was insanely good and I needed some kind of miracle to make it flop.

Gee, miracles! Excellent for my luck has always been just awesome, right?

I zoomed out for clarity because the web of problems I was stuck in was driving me crazy with details, none of them leading to any comforting outcomes.

Then, a sudden realization struck me.

SOOVIN - THE MASTERMIND BEHIND IT ALL

"Why are you even telling me all of this?" I met his proud gaze with my confident one, "Unless, of course...you want me to believe your word for it and do something...If your plan was indeed this bulletproof you would not be telling me all its confidential details. So, I do not believe a single word that you have uttered from your foul mouth"

He pursed his lips, "Not bad, Officer. If you may know, I am telling you all of this because my men are loyal to their bones and ruthlessness is in their blood but intelligence? Not their department. It gets kind of lonely sometimes, you know? Being the only genius in the room whose ideas are not understood by anyone, much less appreciated"

"All you are getting from me are insults, you blockhead," I bit back.

"Oh, don't you worry about that," I was getting sick of his smirks at that point, "The concealed terror on your face is appreciation enough for me, Officer. Besides..."

His eyes acquired a wild spark that made me flinch, "I like my enemies broken beyond measure, both mentally and physically before I suck the soul out of them. However, in your case, it seems like Soovin has already done half of my job"

"He did *not* betray me," I hissed out, looking him right in the eye.

GG laughed, "He has never told you about his family, has he?"

"His family is related to the mafia, I know"

"And?"

My silence was an answer enough for him.

"They had literally placed a bounty of *one million* dollars on your head. In fact, the contract has been active for more than seven years. You were a pretty famous CIA Officer, you know? With almost a thousand enemies. Being the lords of the mafia, they needed to take care of you. When no one could get to you, despite the enormous bounty on your head...they sent their own son to get to you"

I laughed, "You seriously want me to believe that?"

"Oh, I am not done yet, Officer. Give me five more minutes of your precious time and you will see how blind you have acted in those five years you spent with him"

I rolled my eyes at him to hide the effect his words were having on me. I felt as if a distant memory was knocking at my door...A strange yet important memory...Something regarding a phone call...

"Have you ever wondered why Soovin's cases landed at your and only your table when you were in the CIA? Because he *wanted* them to. He was the one who planned *every* little thing about your interactions as a criminal and a CIA Officer. His goal was to get close to you, either win your trust and lure you to his parent's den or blind you with rivalry so much that you happily fall into his trap in hopes of finally catching him. Boy was he succeeding at it!"

GG threw his head backward and laughed merrily, "Then, that little girl came into the picture. Because of reasons beyond my comprehension, Soovin took quite a fancy for her. He suddenly woke up and realized that all of this was 'wrong' and 'fundamentally flawed' in his words. Now, he was yearning to change and start a new life. Then, a genius idea came to his mischievous brain and he saw you as his ticket out of the illegal world. The cherry on top was that you cared about that girl too. You stupid people with your stupid emotions! Like a bonus offer, he got a bodyguard for that girl along with his permit to be free, all in your form, *served to him on a silver platter*"

He leaned forward, shaking his head, "That guy's luck has always been crazy! He resisted his family and put his new plan in action. Telling them lies over lies but how long could have that act lasted? Soovin's family...They are *wild* people, I tell you. Pretty impatient too. After almost four years, they had finally had enough of their good-for-nothing son and told him to come back. When that message reached him, he blocked off all contact with them. So, they naturally reached out to me and told me to knock some sense into him. When I tried to do so, Soovin stabbed me in the back as well, robbed me of my most prized possession, and somehow managed to convince an experienced CIA Officer like you that he wanted to change. Heck, he even convinced you to leave everything behind for him!"

A tear trickled down my cheek but I hid it masterfully.

"That guy has some *serious* tricks up his sleeve. And so he ran away from everything but his family isn't the type to take defeat the right way, much less the betrayal of their own son. However, they still gave him a chance. They found him here while you were having a good month's rest on that hospital bed and presented a clear offer to him- He hands you in and they forget all about his betrayal. Everything would have gone back to normal and they would have been a happy family once again. That persuasive *bastard* even managed to convince them that Anna should be a part of this family! Can you believe it? But here comes the twist. Now, he could not give you to his family easily because that little girl loves both of you as if you were her actual parents. More stupid emotions! So, he turned on his evil brain once again. He happily agreed to his family's offer and was about to hand you in at the hospital with some help from that little burger. After all, Anna would think I took you and so will your brother! No one would even suspect him because he had always pretended to be so nice, friendly, and caring towards you. He would act heartbroken. They will give him only sympathy. The problem would be solved smoothly with all the blame on me. But, I being the generous and kind man I am, stepped in to save the day"

He sighed contently, "Quite a master story, isn't it?"

I shivered from head to toe.

All of this made too much sense...The phone call between Soovin and a mysterious speaker that I had accidentally overheard three years ago just supported GG's theory or rather...*the truth.*

My mind was going hazy with rage and a painful sense of betrayal.

Still, GG didn't need to know that.

My hollow voice trembled as I said, "I don't believe you..."

GG winked at me, "Denial is the first stage of grief, Officer. Don't worry, you'll get over it"

He got up and shut the door behind him, leaving me terror-stricken and horrified to death.

I knew what I needed to do, *If I give myself any time to think, I will break down for sure. I just need to focus on getting out of here.*

I kept on telling myself, *It was all a lie. Soovin did not do that. He did not use you. It's just a well-structured lie. Nothing else.*

One thing I had learned in my CIA training was how to completely shut off my emotions in dire conditions and it was about to come in pretty handy.

I switched my professional mode on, completely ignoring my thoughts that revolved around Soovin, I would have plenty of time to ponder over the story later. I needed to get out of there before Anna came because something about GG's confident smirk told me that she *would* come.

I sighed to myself, "Guess, I need to escape...*again*"

My eyes automatically darted towards the camera and my experienced mind was already scanning the room for blind spots. Sadly, since it was GG we were talking about, there were none. However, I still knew a billion ways to cheat the camera and escape. The only problem was how?

I analyzed the entire room.

It was black-themed and nothing less of a prison cell. A pretty stylish and luxurious prison cell but a prison cell nonetheless. There was just a bed, a table and chair, and a door to a small bathroom which had all possibilities of escape blocked off.

I found nothing that would come in handy to escape.

I muttered, "Guess I'll just have to do what I do best while stressing out"

I reached for my gun, ready to shoot whoever blocked my path to freedom.

To no one's surprise, it wasn't there.

I thought for a bit as a solution presented itself.

GG would be extra cautious and would be watching the CCTV himself all the time after I had already outsmarted him at the helicopter by throwing him outside from 10, 000 feet in the air.

I thought bitterly, *How are his bones not broken at least? Surely he would have suffered some injury before that wrecked chopper saved him, right?*

GG wanted me to be mentally broken. He *expected* me to be mentally broken after Soovin's double cross topped with his plan.

I again shut off the thoughts that this statement had set on fire.

Not now, I told my mind firmly.

I smirked, *Let's give him a show worth watching, then.*

I muttered under my breath, loud enough for the camera's not-so-hidden microphone underneath the right corner of the carpet to hear every word crystal clear, "How could you do this to me Soovin...?"

I wept or so he would think I did.

Pro tip: When you don't find a blind spot, just make one.

In reality, I was trying to get hold of my spare guns attached to both of my legs while shielding my actions from the camera under the impression of having a mental breakdown.

Nothing.

That moron had taken those as well.

I screamed in frustration, partly because it went well with the Oscar-deserving act I was putting up and partly because I was indeed frustrated out of my mind without a gun at my disposal.

While pretending to weep, I checked all the places where I kept my artillery at.

It took me some serious acting skills and a solid amount of time because I mean it when I say, I kept *a lot* of hidden weapons on me.

Minimum 12 knives and 6 guns *at all times.*

I had learned to keep them the hard way in my 7 years of CIA service which was coming more and more handy every minute.

I checked my gun strap. Taken. Knives strapped to the crook of my knees and ankles. Taken. Guns hidden near my elbows. Also taken. Knives between my foot and shoes. Taken Again.

Damn, they really have checked me thoroughly, I thought.

A smirk made its way to my lips, *But not as thoroughly as they should when kidnapping an experienced officer and agent like me.*

I also had a knife strapped to my stomach, just in case and it had been a very clever investment indeed.

I curled up in a ball and pretended to weep even louder. Using my new knife, I tore open the broad soles of my shoes which had a gun and a knife each buried in them.

Was it a bit extra?

Absolutely.

But did it end up saving me?

Absolutely!

Now, I had two fully loaded guns along with three knives. Not bad. In fact, a million times better than being an unarmed prisoner in the base of a madman with an army of mentally sick, barely humane people who were armed to the teeth.

The problem?

I had no idea where to go from there.

Great, I had 2 guns and 3 knives but who could I attack with them? I was an isolated prisoner and the only person I believed would check upon me was GG. He was as trained and experienced as me if not more. Taking over him even with these new weapons would be pretty hard. He knew this place like the back of his hand and thus would have the upper hand if it came down to fighting one on one.

I stuffed my artillery near my waist so that it was still hidden but in reach if I needed to launch some quick attacks.

I finally lifted my face which was buried in my arms for way too long and pretended to wipe my tears. Then, I hugged my knees staring into oblivion, giving the impression that I was wondering the best way to end my life as I thought about my escape plan and mentally said to myself, *Seriously, where is my Oscar at?*

Suddenly, I heard a scraping noise. I looked towards the door to locate its source and found a plate of food being slid to me from under the door.

Even if I had had any appetite, looking at the thing they had the audacity to call 'food' would have made it all go away. Besides, I had been trained to last without food and water for at least a week. So, I was pretty comfortable ignoring the gross items on the plate.

Then, something else caught my eye.

The plate. It seemed to be of pretty strong steel and could act like a temporary bulletproof shield for me.

I made a mental note to launch my attack right after I had been served food so that I had a bullet-stopping plate at my disposal.

I couldn't help but think that if I had been in the CIA, a mere call would have supplied High-tech weapons and armoury to me.

The part of my brain that was still clinging to the emotions of betrayal kept on thinking that Mr. Dune had been right and I should have listened to him. Soovin was not someone to be trusted. He had fooled me and I had let my guard down like a naive.

I thought bitterly, *How could have I not seen through it...? I am such a gullible idiot...I had been ready to die protecting him...I had chosen him and Anna over everything in my life and he...*

It was at that moment, my heart cracked, and performing the weeping became easier than ever for it was no longer an act.

I had pushed down the sense of betrayal engulfing me since Soovin had shown his true colours and right now, it was coming out in an explosion.

I was losing track of time as my tears pooled on the floor, *I left my life behind, my 7 years of successful career in the CIA for him, a back-stabbing assassin...The one and only Officer Hannah Gorgin, the pride of the CIA, fooled by an assassin who knew nothing other than betraying...It was all a mere sinister plot for him, nothing more, nothing less...It was all a lie...a beautiful and deceptive lie...I thought he was healing me but, he broke me even more...*

I felt a hollow pain in my chest, *The first time I went against Mr. Dune, the fatherly figure who I had always looked up to and I am left so broken that I probably won't lower my walls ever again.*

Mr. Dune's heartbreaking words rang in my ear, *The CIA is your home...That pledge of loyalty that you threw away like loose trash, agent?...Agent, don't you think you have been brainwashed by Soovin Cooper...Hannah...Is this really you...?*

For the first time in my entire life, I felt guilty of betrayal myself.

Although at that time I had thought that I was doing the right thing, now, I saw that I had betrayed the CIA when I had sided with Soovin five years ago and karma had just given me a taste of my own medicine.

Although it was unintentional, I had sided with the wrong guy and stabbed the CIA, my own family in the back.

My eyes were getting sore from crying but the tears didn't stop. I didn't want them to. I wanted, I *needed* to let them out.

I was fully aware that while being under the hidden supervision of your enemy, you should appear confident and brave to put yourself in an emotionally superior state than your opponent, but here I was, sobbing on the floor while cursing my rotten luck, revealing all my weak points to my opponent like a fool.

But I couldn't help it.

You need this, I told myself, *Cry as much as you want but make sure that when you are done crying, you never cry for the same reason ever again.*

I let out the final tears as a sense of betrayal and guilt choked me inside.

If there was anything I knew at that point, it was that 'No matter how hard you try and how much you believe in someone, some people never change...Once a betrayer, always a betrayer...'

CHAPTER THIRTEEN

GG's Proposal

After around an hour, I was finally mentally settled and had come to terms with the fact that Soovin was *not* my friend. He had betrayed me purposefully because what better way to keep Anna and himself protected from the CIA than a renowned ex-CIA Officer and agent at his disposal?

He had acted smart and I had fallen right into his trap like a complete naive.

Well, I thought bitterly, *It's not gonna happen again anytime soon.*

At this point, my focus was on escaping once again and not on how unfair life was.

I made a mental note to keep some handcuffs with me as well along with all the guns and knives because if I had had one at the moment, escaping would have been as easy as a pie.

I could have restrained GG with them the next time he decided to show his petty face. He would be restrained and I fully armed which would make up for my lack of information about this place and his thorough knowledge. Hundreds of heavily armed men who would gladly die for GG's protection were a heavy advantage. My only hope was that they would not be foolish enough to attack when I had their Boss at my gun's barrel that too after I had already thrown him from 10, 000 feet in the air.

That would have given them a pretty strong impression of mine which I intended to use as an advantage.

If GG had been watching the cameras, which I was damn sure he was, he would think that I am in an extremely emotionally vulnerable state and his guard would not be as high. It was my best bet.

I had mentally gone through my escape plan and was trying my best to seem more confident than I felt.

Now, all I had to do was wait for the opportunity which I was sure GG would provide me within about an hour due to his overconfidence.

He didn't disappoint me.

The door to my room swung open and GG appeared in front of me with his signature smirk.

I am about to wipe that smirk off your ugly smug face, I thought.

But then, I realized something, he was smiling *triumphantly.* No, scratch that, he was *beaming* with pride and satisfaction.

He entered the room once again and his men closed the door right after.

I took in his appearance.

He was wearing a black shirt with some black jeans along with a black leather belt. No wonder his entire base had black as the only color.

I raised an eyebrow as a plan formed in my mind, *Well, this is convenient.*

"Guess, what happened, Officer?" He said smiling while taking a seat.

I was afraid to ask but I did, "Spit it out, you numskull"

"As cheerful and warm as ever, I see!" He chuckled, "Anyways, the good news is that phase one of my plan has successfully begun!"

I gulped, *This is not good.*

"I had sent two of my men to your lovely trio with a little video of you going bonkers in here"

I acted surprised, "A video?"

He smirked, "There is a camera in here, you see"

He pointed at the clock with the perfectly camouflaged camera which I had already seen the first time I laid eyes on it.

I gasped, "That's an invasion of privacy!"

He snorted, "I have done a billion murders, Officer. An invasion of your petty privacy would not arise any guilt in my conscience"

I acted betrayed and vulnerable as if I didn't already know that he was seeing everything I did in this lockup.

He waved his hand at me, "Save that look for a bit, Officer! You haven't even heard the best part yet. I had voiced in that video that I would gladly trade Anna for you and they had the *audacity* to play that video in front of your pesky little daughter"

I clenched my jaw, *Things are going his way pretty quickly. I need to do something NOW.*

"Also," He continued boasting, "Given the state in which the man's dead body was delivered to me, Soovin is putting up quite an act for the other two of caring about you"

He had figured out my weak point and was trying his best to sprinkle salt over my wound. It took all my mental strength to act nonchalant as if that simple jab didn't make me want to tear him apart and then sob my eyes out while cursing Soovin's name.

He continued pressing my buttons when I didn't budge with the first jab, "That demon is little and naive, I know. But your brother sure is shamefully gullible for a CIA Officer!"

He laughed but stopped abruptly when I smiled.

I leaned closer and whispered, "It's all about *believing* people who have won your trust. Hang on, my bad! How would *you* know about trust and emotional bonds? After all, you are dying to kill the only person who thought of you as his family!"

My laugh seemed to carry my message pretty well, *You aren't the only one good at hitting people's weak points.*

He smirked again but I could see the anger and vulnerability that he was desperately trying to hide.

"Soovin has betrayed both of us, Officer. I might even have formed an alliance with you if it was not for that sharp tongue of yours and your foolishness of messing with me all those years ago"

"Gee! I am dying for us to be a team!" I chuckled with sarcasm dripping from my voice.

His smirk gradually disappeared and he said to me grimly as if he had just realized something, "Officer, I am not kidding. I do have a grudge against you for putting me in that bothersome little cell of the CIA but I escaped from it in barely half a day. My grudge against that swindler is a billion times more powerful and destructive. I want to propose an offer"

I raised my eyebrows as if to say, 'Go on, I am listening'

"It's crystal clear that none of us is fond of the other. However, betrayal by the same person *might just be enough* for us to work together. Think about it, we both are extremely powerful and sophisticated. If we join forces...Soovin won't stand a chance...I am not saying we will be partners forever! I have had a pretty horrible experience with those. All I am saying is...this once, we can work together. Once we have destroyed Soovin, we can go back to our cat and goose chase"

I was speechless.

Never in my wildest dreams had I imagined things to take such a turn. This man had almost killed my mother. I had almost killed him in return when his little helicopter had saved his life. And yet, he was proposing an alliance between us...against Soovin.

I thought, *Am I dreaming? Is a weird hallucination? Or maybe I have finally gone crazy? Yeah, the last one seems pretty possible.*

"You are *not* the kind of psycho to let go of grudges, *especially* small ones," I sighed, "What are you planning?"

He threw his hands in the air defensively, "For once, I am thinking straight, Officer. Your concerns are genuine, no doubt. We both know that after the helicopter incident, things were supposed to get heated between us but...That little fraudster has changed a lot"

I raised my eyebrows skeptically.

He answered my look while waving his hands around to find the right words, "I know that I appear as a...cold-hearted, ruthless, having little-regard-for-life criminal and I am! No doubt about it! But...betrayal is the thing that made me this way, Officer. I wasn't planning on world domination the moment I was born"

He leaned back as if wondering how to put his thoughts into words. Meanwhile, I was in a state of disarray. I had no idea what to do.

Firstly, this cold-hearted psychopath was showing emotions.

God, tell me how was *that* possible?

Secondly, I was actually believing him despite all my rational doubts. What on earth was wrong with me?

And lastly, I was sensing sympathy for him which I should not have but I couldn't help it.

Although he was an evil scoundrel who had himself chosen the wrong path and was rather proud of being the way he was, he *had* been through a lot.

For the first time, I thought about his feelings regarding everything that had happened.

The only person he trusted in the entire world suddenly left his side for 'moral' reasons as Soovin claimed. His story's beginning was almost the same as Soovin's - Hunger and horrible company teaching a child to make a living through all the wrong ways.

If I had forgiven Soovin five years ago by thinking he was merely a misguided child, then didn't GG deserve the same...?

Soovin realized it and turned over a new leaf while he went deeper into the darkness to the point where he was barely humane. They are not the same, The rational side of my brain seemed to say.

"This is how the world works, Officer," For the first time I could hear a tinge of sadness in his voice, "Eat...Or be eaten"

"Change is always an option, you know," I said despite every part of my brain telling me to shut the heck up.

He let out a bitter laugh, "I am aware of that. I don't claim to be a victim, Officer. I *am* a villain and I am happy being that way. Do you know why? Because one has only two choices. Either you boast about your positives and become a hero, a survivor or you get painted as a villain in the so-called 'hero's' story"

I frowned, "What do you mean?"

He laughed but this time, his laugh sounded broken and bitter rather than menacing and overconfident, "You don't know what *actually* happened between me and Soovin all those years ago, do you?"

I looked down and he read my silence, "He has not told you *anything*"

He leaned forward, coming so close to my face that I couldn't help but shiver, "Soovin killed all the people who sided with him out of agony. In a fit of anger, he took a dozen lives of people who believed in him while I fed the ones who like me, thought that the world is too cruel and unfair to stay intact"

He looked me dead in the eye and whispered, "Soovin killed everyone who supported him and became a supposed 'hero' for people who know about our gang split. I placed the family we had created above all, took the pledge to cleanse the earth of people who looked at this family the wrong way, and became an evil creature for everyone...I will burn the world down for my men...they are the only family I *ever* needed..."

I was dumbfounded with no sense of what to do or say. He was changing my perspective of how I viewed everything.

I gathered up the courage and argued back, determined to have the emotional upper hand in the exchange, "Is that why you let Alex die...?"

To my surprise, he smiled, "Who do you think is standing guard at your door at the moment?"

My breath caught in my throat, "It's...him...?"

"This family of mine is the only thing that matters to me, Officer. Whoever threatens its existence...*will* be slaughtered, no matter if it's one...or one hundred"

I brooked no refusal despite the goosebumps forming all over my body, "Don't you think that's a rather self-centred approach and protecting other people's families is just as important as your own...?"

He leaned backward and said with a spark of madness in his eyes, "That is exactly *why* I am the villain, Officer..."

Suddenly, a plate slid inside the room from below the door. It was the cue for me to start my plan but...I began asking myself...do I even need to do all of that...?

Would saying yes to his offer still be fundamentally wrong after what Soovin had done...?

Was it even wrong to betray a betrayer...?

CHAPTER FOURTEEN

Escape Gone Wrong

I had to think fast. I had the perfect chance to escape. GG was here, as emotionally vulnerable as ever. A plate had just been slid inside. My guns and knives were still perfectly hidden yet totally in my reach.

All I had to do was take action but...I hesitated for some reason.

My feelings towards GG were mixed. A moment ago, I would not have batted an eye before shoving my gun's barrel in his mouth and my knife in his throat but now, I was hesitant.

I was no longer sure whether I was on the right side or not.

As I thought about it, I realized that no side was right and no side was wrong. It was not a movie or a children's book going on that there was a clear demarcation between good and evil. This was real life and both sides were grey. One was a lighter shade while the other was a bit darker.

The problem was that the lighter shade was becoming darker and the darker one was becoming lighter with every passing second that I thought about it.

I still had no idea why Soovin had killed the people who had sided with him or who on earth Sharlet was. I was yet to uncover a major part of this backstory and it still seemed too early to decide and I felt too ill-informed to judge but here life was, banging on my doorstep to make a choice.

I was stuck.

So, I decided to listen to the voice inside my head, the voice of Mr. Dune guiding me all those years ago when I was undergoing my CIA training, *There will be times when you are no longer sure which side you are fighting on, Officer. Times when all your sense of judgment will prove to be futile. At that time, to make a decision...all you need to do is ask yourself a basic question. Look deep into your conscience and ask - If it was not for the billion blinding facts and details, if it all came down to trusting someone without any proof or analysis...whose side would you stand by...?*

As soon as I asked the question, an image floated into my mind. An image of me, Soovin, and Anna making forts out of pillows and bed sheets while laughing together. And then an image of me and Soovin promising Anna who was sobbing in my arms in the underground playroom at Spark's demise that we would stand by her side no matter what.

I opened my eyes and knew I had made the right decision.

For a moment, I didn't seem to care that it all had been an act and Soovin had stabbed me in the back just like he had done with GG. All I could think was that *I* was not a betrayer and I would get out of here the right way. If not for Soovin, then for Anna and Frank.

GG raised his eyebrows, "So...what do you think about my offer, Officer? You can take more time if needs be"

I smiled, "Oh, it won't come to that...I have made my decision"

He leaned forward, visibly hopeful, "And it is...?"

My smirk widened as I answered him physically.

With a swift motion, I had grabbed him by the neck. He fell backward along with the chair he was previously sitting on. He thrashed his arms around but I knew I had the upper hand...at the moment at least.

I quickly undid his belt and slid it off. I snapped it on his wrists with a couple of specific motions, making a temporary yet sturdy handcuff that could hold even a giant like him.

He opened his mouth to shout for his guards but I immediately fed him my gun's barrel. That shut him up pretty effectively.

He gulped and a bead of sweat trickled down his neck as the enormity of the situation sank in.

I leaned in close and whispered, "I can end your life by merely pulling the trigger which believe me, my fingers are itching to do"

His eyes darted towards the trigger and my finger placed firmly over it, ready to pull it and take my chances with his men. The look of horror on his face was screaming that he had never been this close to death.

I smirked as I repeated a familiar line, *"The concealed terror on your face is appreciation enough for me, Officer.* That's what you said, right? Do you know what your face screams, right now, Gavin?"

He flinched at the mention of his name but was smart enough to keep his tongue in control or it might have been my gun in his mouth that was preventing him from doing anything other than nod feebly but I did not care in the slightest.

I leaned in close again and smirked, "That you are indeed a *coward* who has the habit of hiding behind his men, treating his so-called 'family' as a temporary shield to be disposed of after use. Do you know why I didn't take your *generous* offer? Because evil is a choice one makes, not a natural state of being. You have made your choice and now, I am going to make mine"

I teased him by lifting and placing my finger on the trigger.

The look on his face was simply priceless and I would have taken a picture of him if I had had my phone with me.

That's a bummer, I thought.

I dragged him up, not making any effort to be gentle with the person because of whom my mom was in the hospital and I was accused of attempting to murder my own mother. I recalled Mom's pale and fragile face to shun any mercy that emerged in my heart.

He doesn't deserve it, my mind seemed to say.

I whispered menacingly in his ear, "Try something and I will shoot your coward mouth and take my chances with your men. You *know* I will"

He clenched his fists trying to contain his rage. This was probably the first time *he* was getting threatened like that and was not the one passing out such threats. The thought warmed my heart.

"Aww..." I mocked him, "Getting angry, are we? Do you want to bite back at me? Try and see what happens"

If looks could kill, I would have been dead. His gaze was not menacing, it was *murderous.* But he sure was smart and didn't advance.

"Now, that's a good boy," I smirked and forced his hands behind his back. My gun was now out of his mouth and aimed at the back of his head.

He hissed, "Officer-"

I lightly pressed the tip of one of my knives into his throat, shutting him up.

"Tell them to open the door," I said.

"If I die, you do too," He frantically tried to reason.

"We both die and my brother and Anna are safe for the rest of their lives. I think I will take *this* offer"

He sighed and said loud and clear, "Open the door"

Two of his heavily armed men opened the door and their jaws dropped at the sight that greeted them. Within a second, their rifles were pointed at me but their faces were terrified and their fingers on the trigger hesitant. I was going to take undue advantage of that.

"That's right, dorks. Fire a bullet and lose this pretty Boss of yours"

"Don't," GG ordered.

"Now, like good children, listen to your Boss and drop those big toys on the ground. Don't you agree, Gavin?"

He gritted his teeth, "Drop the weapons"

And so they did.

I thought, *So far, so good...And I spoke too soon again...*

A dozen armed men rushed towards us and I tightened my grip on GG who was gaining some confidence.

Within a second, more than a dozen guns were pointed at me and I was no longer so confident.

You still have the upper hand, Gorgin, I reminded yourself, *Just stand your ground and don't let even a shred of doubt flicker on your face.*

GG snorted, "See that, Officer? Are you still willing to take chances with my-"

I dug my knife into him so that a tiny droplet of blood came out. Nothing lethal but enough to scare him.

"Did I ask for any suggestions, Gavin?" I asked confidently with a sly smirk.

He gulped.

"Thought so," I said, "Now, you are going to guide me to the exit and *generously* lend me a car, one that lacks any self-destruct mechanisms or..."

I didn't need to finish the sentence for he knew exactly what I could do.

"To the left," He growled helplessly.

His base was stylish and neat but I didn't have any time to appreciate its beauty or even take in my surroundings.

Within a minute, I was staring at an SUV facing the highway with my back towards GG's base.

"It was nice doing business with you," I said getting in the car, my gun still aimed at GG's chest, "Now, if you will do the honours to turn your ugly face around and give me some privacy to start this beauty here"

He clenched his jaw and turned around, his hands still behind his head for he knew better than to play any tricks with me when I was in the zone.

I sighed and tried to calm my racing heart, *It is working. I will be out of here in a moment.*

I stepped towards each one of the cars parked there and slit their tires quietly, thinking, *Try chasing me with those, suckers!*

I took a deep breath, *Now or never, Gorgin.*

In a swift motion, I shut the door of the SUV, started the engine, and shot out of that wrecked base at lightning speed.

I frowned as I saw something familiar from my peripheral view.

I froze on the spot.

I turned around quick enough to snap my neck in half.

My heart nearly stopped at the sight that met me as I screamed a string of curses while smashing the brakes rather harshly.

The tires of the SUV screeched in protest as I dived headfirst into the dashboard but I couldn't even acknowledge the pain or dizziness because my mind was too preoccupied in absorbing the shock I had gotten from what my eyes had seen.

There was Anna, advancing towards GG's base as his men held her at their gunpoint.

Even from a safe distance away, GG's smirk was distinctly visible. I could read the movement of his lips, "The exchange was successful, after all"

CHAPTER FIFTEEN

ANNA SHOWS WHO'S THE BOSS

"REALLY? DON'T YOU HAVE ANY OTHER LIVES TO MESS UP?!" I screamed at the sky

Neither God nor the bright sky gave any sign of hearing me.

My eyes were glued to Anna who was advancing towards GG with a ridiculous amount of confidence for a 15-year-old girl confronting an eccentric criminal.

I took a moment to reflect on my options, my options regarding the way to re-enter GG's den because there was no way in hell I was going to leave Anna there.

I sighed and knew what I had to do.

I turned the car around and slowly approached the dark, black building that seemed to have sucked all the liveliness from its surroundings. I was approaching his base from a side so that they wouldn't get to know about my arrival.

I went over my options once again.

I could just dash there, cause some bloodshed, and take Anna out with me but it was highly unlikely that I would succeed. After the way I had insulted GG with my escape, he was guaranteed to be fuming with rage and yearning for revenge. He would probably shoot Anna the second I am in sight and ruin his plan just to get back at me.

Yup, that sounds exactly like what he would do, I thought while slowing the car down for I was about to reach there without being mentally prepared in the slightest.

I could try for a surrender but I knew he would never believe that and the same procedure would follow.

My only options were stealth and intelligence.

I muttered while parking the car discreetly in the midst of some lively, green bushes that contrasted with the dull and gloomy outskirts of the building, "Well, it's about time...I was starting to get a bit rusty"

I crept closer to all the people while hiding behind one of the SUVs with slit tires.

Not the best hiding spot, I agree but it was my odds-on-favorite to survive myself and rescue Anna. Besides, all of the men were pretty occupied staring at Anna who was so confident one might have thought she was making a business deal with GG and not being carried as a hostage.

I could hear her brave demand break the silence, "Where is my mom?"

GG's mouth split open in a grin, "Remember me, do you? Both mother and daughter have a mutual hatred for proper introduction and humble greetings, I suppose?"

Anna folded her arms across her chest bossily.

I could see GG's men trying their best not to look puzzled, awestruck, or let a smile loose. I myself was struggling to keep a proud smirk at bay.

GG shook his head and muttered to himself, "What on Earth is wrong with this family?!"

Anna's lips slowly gave way to a smirk.

GG turned around and ordered, "Bring this kid inside into the hall"

"This *kid* has legs, mister, and knows very well how to walk," Anna scowled and followed GG, not seeming to be worried at all.

GG sighed irritatedly but decided to control his frustration.

He pointed at an armed female, "You, stand guard here in case *our dear friend* somehow decides to return"

"Yes, Captain," She saluted and took her position.

"Rest of you," GG continued, "Keep an eye on this vexing little girl, here. If she is somehow gone, you all will be too"

There was a collective, classic, 'Yes, Captain'

GG advanced inside.

One of the men attempted to hold Anna's arm firmly to prevent any potential escape but she shook him off harshly and gave him a withering look.

He gulped and followed her from a safe distance. When a 15-year-old girl gives you *that* look, you should do the same.

They all were going inside and I knew I needed to blend in to follow them, the question was how?

Suddenly, the lady standing guard caught my eye. There was a cap on her head, whose front visor could easily hide the wearer's face.

I raised my eyebrows, *Well, it's not like she is completely innocent...Borrowing her cap for some time won't do any harm...probably.*

With a quick death touch, I had a new cap which did a wonderful job of hiding my face. Plus, it matched the caps of several others, so, I could easily blend in without arousing much suspicion.

I quietly followed the pack of loyal, armed hounds at GG's heel. I was blending in pretty well for none of the hundred or so people glanced at me twice.

Not that I was paying much attention to anyone except Anna.

She appeared brave but I knew how freaked out she was by the way she walked.

It took everything in me not to grab her and make a run for it.

Be patient and wait for the right moment, I told myself, *DO NOT mess this up.*

We entered a hall that was built like a medieval throne room.

I controlled the urge to roll my eyes, *Why am I not surprised?*

GG sat down on the large throne that would have belonged to the king if this had been an actual palace and not a creepy mansion. Anna stood in front of him, her hands on her hips.

He smirked, "Look who has decided to-"

"Where. Is. My. Mom?" Anna asked with threateningly big eyes.

I wanted to shake her awake at this point.

I was mentally screaming, *WHO DOES SHE THINK SHE IS TALKING TO?! THAT IS A DANGEROUS MAN WITH HIS ENTIRE MENTAL TOOLBOX MISSING, NOT AN OLD FRIEND!*

"Careful, young one," GG growled as his men shivered from head to toe for they knew that tone of voice all too well, "Cutting me off has cost people their lives-"

"Don't make me ask the same question more than twice," She narrowed her eyes.

At this point, GG looked more confused than ferocious.

He scowled at her, "Do you even know who I am?"

Anna shrugged casually, "I do. I just don't care. My mom and dad are going to make you a dead man soon, anyway"

I barely controlled my laughter and thought, *I raised her SO well...*

GG seemed to have regained his playfulness, "Aww...Is that so? God, you are *so* delusional..."

"Come to the point, will you?" Anna said hotly.

GG leaned forward in his chair and said with a smirking face, "Your dear mother...is dead"

I almost gasped, *WHAT THE HECK-*

"Oh what a shame," Anna threw her hands in the air with a bored look on her face.

"You think I am joking?" GG said infuriated.

Anna mimicked puking and at this point, I just knew I had raised her incredibly well, "Sorry, I am allergic to horrible jokes"

She rolled her eyes at him and even I was starting to admire her courage, her *foolish* confidence that could end up killing us all but confidence nonetheless.

"You want to know how that arrogant mother of yours died? She was this overconfident as well and took me for granted, much like you. I shot her right in the skull," GG shrugged casually.

"Show me the body then," Anna said.

I smiled to myself thinking, *Busted by a fifteen-year-old girl.*

But to my surprise, GG smiled and clapped his hands.

Then...a dead body was brought in...*my* dead body.

I had never been more confused in my life. The body looked exactly like me and I barely fought the urge to prick myself somewhere to see if blood came out and to confirm whether I was a human or a ghost.

Mind twisting is his cup of tea, I told myself, *Believe in your mind, not what your eyes see.*

For a moment, Anna looked panicked and frightened but she composed herself almost immediately. She advanced towards my dead body and traced my jawline with the tip of her finger.

Then, she pulled off the face mask that revealed someone else's face.

She turned around and threw the mask towards GG who caught it just in time with a menacing and wild gaze.

She shrugged as if disappointed, "Would you look at that? The man with the entire underworld at his fingertips can't even fool a fifteen-year-old girl, it's really such a shame"

If it was not for the dire circumstances, I would have started applauding her right there and then. I was feeling more and more proud of her with every passing minute.

GG clenched his jaw and gritted out, "Beginner's luck"

Anna actually chuckled and said, "You want to know how I knew? I might not have come crazy training in this field of work but I *know* my mom and believe me she can take an army of a hundred such people and still classify it as 'light work'. *You* are no match for her"

Alright, I thought, *We need to have a talk after all this. She has severely overestimated my capabilities and hearing her wordings, I just know which blue-eyed blond idiot is to blame.*

I also made a mental note to tell him to stay away from my daughter.

GG hissed, "Is that so?"

He pointed towards me and my heart stopped.

All I could think was, *Well, I still have 2 guns and 3 knives. I should be able to win this.*

But then, he pointed towards two other men and said, "YOU, YOU AND YOU, take this bothersome little delusional kid to the cell. RIGHT NOW!?"

I mimicked the other two men's behaviour and saluted GG while gagging behind my cap in disgust.

Then, along with the two soon-to-be-dead morons, I marched Anna towards whatever 'cell' these two were walking towards as a smirk crept on my lips, *Well, this is going to be fun...*

THE JINXED HUGS

"Walk faster," One of the men told Anna to which she replied by slowing to a crawl.

He pointed his gun's barrel at her which was his first mistake, "I said *walk faster*"

Instinctively, I smacked his hand harshly and the gun fell to the floor.

He looked daggers at me, "What are you-?!"

"Following the orders," I said curtly in a masked voice with a fake accent.

"She is right," The other guy added, "Captain won't be happy if your finger fails to obey you and you know very well what he would do then"

"Fine," He gritted out and looked at Anna with disgust and hatred, "BUT IF YOU DON'T MOVE FAST, YOU LITTLE-"

That was his second and last mistake.

Within a blink of an eye, I had silently death-touched the other guy and had this shot-tempered idiot pinned down with my knife pressed into his throat.

"WHAT-"

I pressed the knife further, silencing him. His eyes went wide with shock and fear when he saw my face.

I said in my usual voice, "No one, and I mean *no goddamn person* talks to my daughter that way that too in front of *me*"

"Mom...?" Anna said in disbelief.

With my back towards her, I silenced the man forever. I then, turned around to see her.

"Miss me, ha?" I smiled as her jaw dropped to the floor.

She engulfed me in a hug and as much as I loved her, I was getting sick of this kind of hug because every time we hug after we reunite some crap goes down and it is once again a separated, near-death experience.

I pulled back as the thought occurred to me and flashed her a comforting smile.

Suddenly, I heard a scream, "CAPTAIN, IT'S HER! BOTH OUR MEN ARE DOWN!"

"I am starting to think these hugs are jinxed," I muttered as I shot the screaming idiot in the leg for my CIA side still didn't permit me to kill men, even criminals unless it's completely necessary...or I am *really* pissed off.

"THERE THEY ARE!" Another man screamed.

Without uttering a single word, I grabbed Anna's hand and started running down strange and unfamiliar corridors. There was only one thing on my mind, *We need to hide.*

"MOM, STOP-"

"There is no time, Anna," I snapped under pressure while my mind went, *WHAT ARE WE GOING TO DO IF WE RUN INTO A DEAD END?! WHAT IF GG IS WAITING FOR US IN THE NEXT CORRIDOR?! WHAT IF THEY SHOOT RIGHT NOW?! WHAT IF-*

"Shut up," I huffed and then glanced apologetically at Anna's sad face, "Not talking to you, sweetheart"

We ran into an open room with a bed. I quickly shut the door but did not bolt it for it will only raise suspicion and would not stop those giants from breaking in.

I got down on my knees and gestured Anna to do the same. Much to my disappointment, she saw right through it.

"You are *not* pushing me under the bed again," She argued.

"Yes, I am," I said while looking under the bed.

All safe, my mind reported.

"NO-"

I quickly covered her mouth and whispered, "Jeez! Keep it down if you don't want them to barge in!"

She took a deep breath as if finally understanding, I removed my hand from her mouth and she said faintly but firmly, "No"

I threw my hands into the air, "OH MY GOODNESS, ARE YOU KIDDING ME?!"

She narrowed her eyes at me, "Didn't you just tell me to keep it down?"

I rubbed my face which was red with panic, thinking, *Oh boy, this is not going to be easy.*

I sighed and looked at her right in the eyes, authoritatively, "Anna, it is already pretty damn bad. *Please* don't make this harder"

"And where will you go, ha?! We are *not* separating with all those on our tails," She said and for a moment I saw a flicker of resemblance on her face.

This is exactly what Soovin would have said, I thought spontaneously.

I flinched at the sudden emotional jab. Just what I needed with hundreds of men searching for us both like hounds. Perfect. Thanks a lot, supportive life.

Anna continued in a tone that made it pretty clear that she wouldn't budge, "Either we both go under the bed, or no one does. As simple as that!"

I sighed defeatedly.

She smiled triumphantly.

"This is *freaking* ridiculous..." I muttered while aiming both my guns at the door from under the bed and shaking my head.

Anna smirked and said in a horribly mimicked tone, "Anna is here, will you *kindly* mind your *bloody language!?*"

I bit my lip and muttered under my breath, "If Mr. Dune saw me like this...he would probably book me a room in the asylum after stating the billion things that make this the worst attacking position in history..."

"You know, talking to yourself is one of the first signs that you need asylum," Anna held her laughter.

I grunted, "Cut the cackle, will you?"

She replied, "By the way, you don't need to panic, Uncle and Dad-"

Anna was cut off when someone barged inside the room.

I gripped my gun tighter and took out my knives as well.

The man seemed to be searching the room for *someone.* He looked at all the prime hiding places in a hurry.

Then, to my horror, he knelt down and his body twisted towards our not-so-safe hiding spot.

My grip on my gun tightened even more, making my knuckles go white with effort.

My mind started running at lightning speed once again as adrenaline surged through my body, *I have to shoot him before he announces our presence to the other men...but...the sound of the gunshot would bring them here nonetheless. Knives are a better option...but they won't kill him instantly and give him enough time to call for backup. I need to use the knife on his throat, the second he sees us. That's the only option that doesn't end with us tied at GG's feet.*

I could feel Anna scoot closer to me for some comfort but I didn't dare look away from the man's body.

Any second now, I thought.

Just when the man was about to come into my view, another person barged inside and I divided my attention between the two.

Even the man who had almost discovered us turned around, "What?"

The guy who had just entered panted, "Cap...Captain...called...urgent..."

I could hear the frustration in his voice when he said, "Really?! What could be more urgent than that bloodthirsty lioness lurking around here with her little cub?"

I smiled, *At least they know who they are dealing with.*

The other man finally caught his breath, "Captain has ordered everyone in the hall, NOW!"

The man got up and I felt Anna relax beside me, "Emergency level? It can't be more-"

"12," came the reply immediately.

This was followed by a stunned silence. The guy seemed shocked and we were confused.

I am getting sick of their codes and emergency levels, I thought, *Would it be too much to ask for a guide with their stupid numbers and meanings?*

The first guy broke the silence, "Are you sure you didn't mishear it?"

"Damn sure," his tone was grim.

Whatever is going on, it doesn't seem very good for me, I thought bitterly.

"But..." The guy seemed thunderstruck, "What's the code number?"

The guy sighed deeply, "Code 121"

"Doesn't that mean-"
"Soovin was spotted approaching the base"
I mentally cursed, *Just what I need right now. Soovin.*

THE SQUAD REUNITES

Both of them went rushing out. I and Anna got out from under the bed.

"See," She said, "I was trying to tell you that Uncle and Dad are coming but you won't listen-Are you fine, Mom?"

I snapped back from my not-so-bright thoughts and flashed her a smile, "Yeah, of course"

She placed her hands on her hips, "How many times do I need to tell you that you are a horrible liar?"

"We don't have time for this, Anna. All of his people would be there. I need to get to the hall. Frank would need help-"

"Woah," She showed her palms, "*We* need to get to the hall and Dad is also coming with Uncle-"

"I am not hard of hearing, Anna!" I snapped back unintentionally.

She narrowed her eyes at me, "Are you sure you are fine? You don't seem very fine"

I took a deep breath to calm the anger rising in my chest, "Sorry, my bad. Also, you are indeed coming with me because I can't risk leaving you alone in this madman's base but you will not be jumping in any of the action, got it?"

She rolled her eyes, "Whatever"

Another suspicion crept into my mind, "How did they know where to come? Who told them GG would keep both of us at the base and not play some sick game?"

"Actually...They didn't allow me to come...So, I left a note behind for them to track my location using this," She lifted her wrist and showed me my bracelet.

"Should've figured that out," I muttered under my breath, "That was a smart yet incredibly foolish move, Anna. You should *not* have done this"

"But I came for you!" She argued.

"I had already escaped! I had to come back to get you!" I exclaimed.

"Oh..." She went speechless for a while for she knew it was her fault now, "Well...I didn't know that"

I peeked outside by opening the door a fraction, "What did you plan on doing, anyway? Come here, fight off the guards yourself, and save the day? Or did you think GG would actually keep his word and trade me for you? Stupid teenagers..."

"Hey, I am not that foolish!" She peeked over my shoulder, "Dad was already ready to barge in here and search for you but he talked about the security of the base in detail first. So, Uncle wanted us to go in after some proper planning but Dad couldn't wait. So, I secretly freed the man who had brought the video, well the one left *alive* of the two who had come. Then, I came here with him. That way Uncle would be forced to hurry up and Dad was already ready to come to your rescue"

"Bet he was," I muttered bitterly.

He had planned it all so well. First, he announced the dangers so that Frank would pressurize on planning and he could act like he wanted to free me and yet stay out of any danger. A backstabber or not, he was wickedly clever, I would give him that.

"What was that?" Anna asked.

"Nothing," I gritted out, "Let's just sneak towards the hall. Frank would be there soon and I don't intend to let him face the entire army alone"

"Dad *is* with him"

That is exactly why I don't want him to be alone. Soovin could bite back, I thought, *How do I even tell you this?*

I quietly got out of the room, still hidden behind a big vase, while keeping an eye on the way all the men were going for I had no idea what on earth was the way to this hall.

"Okay, hang on, why are you avoiding the topic of Dad?" Anna asked the question I had no intention of answering.

"I am not avoiding the topic of your Dad," I replied without any emotion, my eyes trained on the men swarming down a hallway.

"He has a name, you know?"

"We are in grave danger, you know? Not the idle time to chat," I started following the group from a safe distance.

Anna was on my heel, "Okay, but-"

I covered her mouth hastily and hid both of us behind a corner as one of the men turned around.

"I think I saw someone there," his voice met my ears as my heart pounded in my ears.

I heard several guns loading and made an attempt to creep around with Anna...only to find another group of men there.

We were trapped. Badly.

On one side, there were five men and on the other, there were twelve.

Five it is, I thought as I loaded my gun and readied the knives once again.

I looked at Anna, *No one should lay a finger on her but I can't take down five men while carrying her...I need to be extremely quick or this would prove to be a suicide attempt.*

I took a deep breath and jumped around the corner.

Before they could react, I threw my knives at three of them and then, covered the mouths of the other two giants. They were putting up quite a fight and I couldn't kill them with both of my hands occupied with covering their mouths.

I am screwed, I thought, *Now I have to move. They will alert other men but I don't have an option.*

I said a silent prayer.

Then, I moved my hand and used my knife as fast as I could but as usual, I wasn't fast enough for the guy had already let out a scream.

I cursed and sent the other guy to permanent sleep as my mind worked, *New priority: Grab Anna and make a run for it.*

I turned around and froze on the spot.

"Move an inch closer and she is going to pay the price," The man said while pressing a knife to Anna's throat to emphasize his point.

It took everything in me to stay rooted to the spot. Anna looked petrified.

"We both know you can't kill her for you dear Boss wants her alive," I said confidently as if my stomach wasn't doing summersaults.

"But we both also know that he wouldn't mind a few scratches here and there," He bit back and gestured for a man to step toward me.

I sighed defeatedly but my eyes remained fixated on the millimetre of the gap between the knife's sharp edge and Anna's tender skin.

I almost said aloud, *If you move that a nanometre closer to her, I will chop you into pieces,* but then decided against it as it would only announce my desperation for him to exploit.

Instead, I held my hands up, admitting defeat...for now.

The guy pointed his gun at my head and pushed me forward. I let him.

I winked at Anna secretively and barely resisted a smirk when I realized where they were bound to take us.

I should have thought of this earlier. This is a much more convenient way to the hall, I thought while pretending to be scared and fuming whenever any one of them glanced at me.

We were taken to the same hall where Anna had made GG go purple with rage.

GG stood with a proud smirk, "Sneaky little cat, aren't you Officer?"

"Nosy little failure, aren't you Gavin?" I snapped right back before I could stop myself.

I made a promise to myself, *Once we are out of this mess, I am going to join some anger management classes.*

He stomped towards me while growling, "If you don't hold your tongue-"

I stomped towards him with equal anger and frustration if not more, "If you talk about cutting anyone's tongue once again, I am going to chop off your-"

"FREE THEM NOW!" A familiar scream cut me off.

Within a tenth of a second, all the guns were pointed at Frank whose gun was pointed at GG.

"What a pleasant surprise!" GG laughed, "Now I can take all of you down in one single swoop. Thanks a lot for that

Officer Frank"

"Not so fast," A painfully familiar voice came from beside GG.

Soovin had suddenly popped up behind him with a gun. Even GG was taken aback by his sudden appearance.

He tried to turn back but Soovin pressed his gun into him.

I couldn't take my eyes off Soovin, *How could he act so damn good?*

His lingering gaze settled on me and he passed me a smile. However, his smile turned into a frown when he saw my betrayed and rageful look that probably screamed, 'I WANT TO RIP YOU APART, YOU LITTLE RAT!'

I took a deep breath to calm my nerves, *Not now, Gorgin...I really should have enrolled for some anger management classes before all of this.*

"Soovin," GG chuckled, "How do you manage to surprise me every goddamn time, buddy?"

Soovin turned his attention to GG and said with a smug look, "You haven't changed much of the base, have you?"

GG laughed, "How many secrets have you buried here, ha?"

"Loads," Soovin's eyes darkened, "But we don't have much time to go through them, do we?"

He pressed his gun further and growled, "Order your men to release them"

"Aww...Such a sweet-"

Soovin loaded his gun, "Now"

"I thought you went clean. Innocent civilians don't kill people, you know?"

"Certain people like you might have prevented me from changing altogether," He replied, "I *will* press the trigger if you don't tell your men to leave them alone"

Frank joined the conversation, "I am going to approach each of them one by one to make sure you are done playing games. If any of your men try to stop me or harm them..."

Soovin completed while tapping his gun, "You very well know what is going to happen"

Frank approached Anna and whispered something in her ear.

She replied back in a whisper and Frank declared, "Yup, it's her"

Then, he approached me and despite the unpropitious circumstances and a hundred guns pointed at us, I smiled on seeing him, "How many times shall I tell you I don't appreciate you having secrets with Anna? I am just beginning to discover the things you tell her. Who the heck told you that I can take an army of a hundred people and still classify it as 'light work' ?"

His composed face broke into a grin and he shrugged playfully, "Well...it's not *not true*"

Then, his smile disappeared and was replaced by a grim look.

He lowered his voice to a faint whisper hearing which made my jaw drop to the floor, "Han...Mr. Dune has betrayed the CIA"

ESCAPED...ALMOST

Frank continued in an urgent and secretive manner, "He is-"

I scowled, "More like your pea-sized brain has become even more gullible. Will you *ever* grow up, blondie? That is the most horrible and foolish lie. I can't believe you fell for-"

"Yeah, it's *definitely* her," he declared and flashed me a wink.

I rolled my eyes as an involuntary smile made its way to my face as well.

Damn...He WAS getting good at this, I thought.

"Great," my smile disappeared on hearing Soovin's voice as I felt another wave of betrayal wash over me.

This one was more rageful than gloomy but I somehow managed to keep myself in control.

"You guys are getting a bit rusty," GG laughed, "That just gave me enough time to do some things"

Now, everyone's smile had disappeared except GG.

Uncertainty flashed on Soovin's face as he demanded, "What are you-"

Two of GG's men threw themselves on Soovin who lost his balance and got buried under the giants. GG lunged towards Anna with a glistening knife that he had snatched from the man nearest to him.

Without a thought, I lunged towards Anna as well, faster than him. I swiftly pushed her towards Frank who caught her immediately.

However, in doing so, I had exposed my back to my opponent, that too with both my arms ready to be held in a firm grip.

GG assessed the situation in a matter of seconds and amended his plans. He gripped my hands behind my back and pressed the knife to my throat while facing Soovin.

I cursed under my breath.

I knew exactly what he was thinking. Even if Soovin had betrayed me, he wouldn't let Anna see any bloodshed. Also, he had kept his act up in front of Anna and Frank and would probably try to keep it up some more to reap benefits in the future.

"Damn, you are clever," I couldn't help but mutter.

"You should have taken my offer when you had the chance, Officer," He said.

Soovin's eyes widened, "Han, what offer is he talking-"

GG pulled my head backwards rather harshly, "Return it to me or she dies...And after a moment, so will Anna"

"WHAT DO YOU WANT?!" Soovin thundered.

"The thing you stole from me buddy, right before stabbing me in the back, might I add," GG said smugly.

Soovin sighed dejectedly, "Look...I don't have it..."

GG pressed the knife further.

"Not at the moment!" Soovin added hastily.

I could feel the tip of the cold metal pressing into my throat.

Still, the scariest part was how unafraid I felt. I was seriously getting concerned regarding my mental health at that point. I *could* dieand all I could think was, *He can't even afford to kill me right now...Dang it!*

Soovin inhaled sharply.

GG growled, "I. Want. It. Back"

He replied threateningly with his eyes fixed on the tip of the knife that was pressing into my skin, "Look, I am trying my best to be civil but if you move that knife a centimetre closer to her, *I will tear you apart, limb by limb*"

I couldn't hold my irritation any longer and scowled at him, "Drop the act, will you?"

He frowned, his face laced with confusion that almost looked genuine, "Han...what are you...?"

Then, his eyes widened as if a sudden realization had hit him in the face. I could feel his eyes stare at GG with indescribable rage and a hint of desperation as if his worst fears had come true.

He gritted out with a clenched jaw, "What the hell did you *tell her,* Gavin?"

Even though I couldn't see GG for he was holding my hands behind my back in a tight grip, I *knew* he was smirking when he said, "What you were too afraid to...*coward*"

Frank said uncertainly, "Umm...On the behalf of almost everyone here, what the heck are you two talking about? I just feel like we all are *not* on the same page"

"Yeah, what are you guys talking about?" Anna piped in.

"Oh nothing," I shrugged as my mind went into professional mode, "Just about Sharlet"

GG tensed as he was taken back by surprise.

My masterstroke had worked.

His composure had fumbled only for a second but that was all I needed.

I side-stepped with lightning speed and switched our positions.

Now, he was the one with a knife at his throat while I was the one with a dozen or so guns pointed at my head.

"Watch it, you morons," I said while securing my grip over GG as well as the black knife, "We *have* done this before and I will need you to cooperate with me once again or things might get *way* uglier than last time"

GG growled, more in frustration than in anger.

"Getting sick of it, are you?" I smirked.

"Oh, you bet," He grunted while struggling against my firm and well-placed grip on his hands.

"Well then...Get better at what you do and things like this might not happen twice in a day. Honestly, are you waiting for me to order you around with more insults?"

He took the hint and growled, "Drop the guns"

His loyal men followed his orders without any hesitation.

I didn't move my eyes from GG for I knew he would try to pull something off again, "Frank, get Anna and everyone out of here, I'll follow along"

Soovin said exasperated, "I am not *everyone*, Han. I do have a name-"

I purposefully ignored him altogether, along with the hundred or so people staring at me as if they would rip me apart with their bare hands if GG gave them the green light to do so, "Also, how the heck did you reach here?"

"Psychopaths aren't the only ones who have access to helicopters, now, are they?" Frank smirked proudly, "I have...*borrowed* a helicopter from the CIA"

"A little chat on borrowing things that way from the CIA later, once we are safely on the way back to...honestly, anywhere would be better than here. Get yourself and these two in that helicopter. I will follow along with the clumsy crime lord who has no idea how to do his job"

I smirked at the jab and GG growled but decided to stay silent.

Once again, I crawled towards the gate with GG at my gunpoint as Frank and *other people* lead the way.

My jaw dropped on seeing the helicopter and GG snickered at my gunpoint, "This is your vehicle of choice?"

"You came here in *this?*" I asked Frank in disbelief, "This looks a breath away from falling apart. Can this thing even take off?"

"HEY!" Frank protested, "It was the easiest to take from the headquarters without raising suspicion. It had no security at all"

"Gee! I wonder why that is..." I remarked sarcastically.

"We don't have any more options, do we? Unless you are willing to borrow one of this idiot's self-destructing helicopters again," Frank bit back.

GG growled, "Watch it, Officer-"

"I'll honestly prefer that over this *ancient legacy*," I muttered under my breath but added, "Get on quickly, will you? I will be flying, no arguments"

He just shook his head at me.

When the three of them were safely packed inside the helicopter, I advanced towards the pilot's seat.

I muttered into GG's ear, "Goodbye, see you *never*"

He smiled in a way that sent shivers down my spine, "Officer, we both know that is not going to be the case. I'll come...Don't you worry about that..."

I pushed him forward and climbed into the pilot's seat with my gun still steadily aimed at him. Then, I dropped my aim and immediately slammed the door shut.

The second GG was out of my gun's reach, thousands of bullets smacked the helicopter and I fumbled with the controls.

"HAN, QUICK! THIS HELICOPTER ISN'T THE STRONGEST!" Frank screamed over the deafening bullet shots.

"THANKS FOR POINTING THAT OUT, SHERLOCK!?" I screamed back in frustration.

The helicopter started at a snail's pace and I abused its controls beyond measure to get some speed in the startup. It's metal parts screeched in protest.

Part of me was sure that this old man would crumble into pieces before taking off but the rusty helicopter did rise up...with a lot of chittering throughout its body.

I tightened my grip on the controls and took a deep breath to make up for all my doubts, "Hey, I was one of the best pilots in my unit. I did races with Mr. Dune himself! How hard could flying this kid be?"

Turns out, it *was* hard.

I pressed the controls. Nothing. I pulled with all my strength to get the helicopter up before the bullets shredded all of us.

Then, it moved...a lot.

I almost fell out of my seat because of the impact like Frank while the helicopter jerked upwards. Its controls were anything *but* smooth.

Surprisingly enough, I managed to steer it away from the creepy cult with guns.

"I think we might actually make it," I said triumphantly while glancing backwards...when I saw an actual CIA helicopter advancing towards us.

"OH COME ON!?" We all groaned together.

"How am I supposed to outrun their shining new model with this piece of garbage?!" I screamed as I concentrated on the controls once again.

"Han..." I could hear fear and apprehension in Frank's voice, "I don't think you could outrun that even with the same model...The pilot is Mr. Dune"

MR. DUNE KNOWS

I looked back so suddenly that I almost heard my neck snap.

Frank handed me his pair of binoculars.

I got up while putting the helicopter on auto-pilot, "HOW IS THIS EVEN POSSIBLE? Unless...Frank, was Mr. Dune around when you stole the helicopter?"

"No one was!" Frank replied in panic.

"He is an ace at hiding when he needs to do so..." I muttered as I pushed the wreckage of a helicopter to its absolute limits.

They would catch up in a minute or so and we needed a plan before their arrival.

"There are two options," I said to no one in particular, "Either everyone except Frank has to hide or Frank himself has to hide because there is no way in hell we are outrunning that helicopter and disclosing that Frank is on our side is the last thing we need right now"

"Frank, hide!" Soovin said.

"Where, may I ask?" He replied sarcastically.

We all frantically looked around. There was absolutely nothing that could hide a full-grown human like Frank.

Then, an idea came to my mind.

But it will take too much time and they should come into view in 30 seconds at maximum, My inner critic said.

There is no other way...but we are short on time. I need something to buy us time, I thought.

Then, out of the blue, I turned the helicopter around back to GG's base.

"HAN, WHAT ARE YOU DOING?!" Soovin screamed as he fell to the floor, taken by the momentum. I was tempted to take another sharp turn just to watch that again but I already had quite a lot on my plate to take care of.

"HAN, WHY ARE YOU GOING BACK TO THAT LUNATIC?!" Frank screamed over the chittering of the ancient helicopter.

"FRANK, COME HERE!" I said urgently as my eyes spotted a handcuff and duct tape in a box near the controls.

Frank approached me with his face laced with concern that almost made me reconsider my decision, "You need help with something?"

With my one hand on the controls of the helicopter and the other advancing toward the box, I looked him dead in the eye and said sincerely, "My deepest apologies for what's about to happen"

His eyes widened as it dawned on him, "HAN, NO-"

I taped his mouth as gently as possible and put the handcuffs on his wrists. He kept on saying something but his voice was muffled beyond comprehension by the duct tape.

"Look, I am not enjoying this either...well maybe a little-"

He tried to smack me with his cuffed hands and somehow succeeded.

I continued, "The point is we don't have many options. My unexpected turn has bought us only a few seconds which is not enough to find a hiding place for a giant such as you. So, just...keep thrashing around, trying to smack me and stuff. You need to put up a show good enough to elude Mr. Dune"

If looks could kill, I would have died right there and then. Frank was trying his best to eat me up with his gaze which was good for my plan but not very helpful when I was trying to concentrate on controlling the disobedient helicopter.

"Agent," A familiar deep voice met my ears, "Officer Frank-What are you doing...?"

I made a conscious effort to keep my mouth shut.

Soovin said, "Han, don't listen to him!"

I flinched. He *had* to choose this moment to talk to me after all that he had done.

"Don't tell me what to do," I hissed back before I could control myself.

Mr. Dune raised his eyebrows.

He was a quick-witted guy and it was a child's play for a face reader of his potential to figure out what was going on just by looking at my face.

"I told you, didn't I...?" was all he said but he and I both knew exactly what he was talking about.

"I..." Nothing else came out of my mouth as my lips betrayed me...just like Soovin had.

His eyes showed warm sympathy, "Still, all is not lost, Agent...You can mend it all...This is your last chance"

"I *betrayed* the CIA..." I whispered, more to myself than anyone.

"Han..." I heard Soovin's heartbreaking whisper of disbelief.

I saw Mr. Dune's composure break as if he was getting affected by the flood of emotions I was drowning in. After all, he had always treated me like family, way more than simply an officer or agent working under him.

"We can fix it, Hannah...Believe me, we still can," His voice trembled at the end.

He had called me by my name only once before this...on *that* night.

At that moment, I asked myself, *Is it really too late to return to the CIA...? I could have my old life back...All of it...*

"Mom..." I heard Anna whisper in a tearful voice.

I shook from head to toe, *I couldn't do this...I promised her...*

Her faint whisper seemed to have broken the trance I was in, *Was I really considering leaving both of them NOW, when they needed me the most? Something is grossly wrong with me.*

My mind quickly went into professional mode again. *THANK GOD FOR THAT*, I thought.

Now, my priorities were straight - Escape the CIA or more accurately escape a shiny and fast model of helicopter with Mr. Dune as the pilot with this piece of absolute trash.

That was impossible. No doubt about it.

So, I had to take a smart and sneaky approach...complicated and deceiving enough to elude Mr. Dune...Next to impossible but I had to try for I had no other choice.

"Is it still possible to back all the way up to five years?" I asked, my voice filled with emotions while my mind worked hastily to craft a plot.

He gave me his undivided attention and his frown slowly eased, "Yes, Officer. I assure you. I will have all the charges over you cleared"

I pretended to go through an inner struggle while the gears of my mind refused to turn in the face of adversity.

"I get where you are coming from agent...I...I looked into Henry Spark's history"

Mr. Dune glanced at Soovin and Anna and then continued with his face towards me, "This guy...he might not be the culprit of that case, I will give him that. Let's even assume he is willing to turn over a new leaf, if all of this is not some sinister plot for him but..."

For the first time, Mr. Dune glanced at Soovin with a sad look of understanding and helplessness instead of a poisonous look, "If circumstances come to the rescue of a criminal...it does not guarantee his innocence forever"

"I am *not* a criminal," Soovin gritted out and I could hear the tears in his voice.

I of all people knew how much he loathed being classified as a 'criminal' but lately...I had been asking myself...was he really not one at all?

My head was spinning.

If my failure at coming up with a plan wasn't frustrating enough, I was still going through an inner turmoil.

A part of me was seething with rage and demanded vengeance for betrayal while a small yet certain part of me somehow still believed Soovin was innocent and that he had *not* betrayed me.

After all, GG is a pro at mind-twisting and clever enough to give rise to a powerful delusion, it seemed to say in its defence.

Not now, I scolded myself, *We NEED a plan.*

My mind seemed to reply, *It's impossible. Pray to God to forgive your sins. That's all you can do.*

You are useless, I almost screamed out loud.

I was a bit puzzled, *Am I seriously calling myself useless...?*

"Agent...This is your last chance. It's your and only your choice. You need to make a decision...now," Mr. Dune said with certainty.

I glanced at Soovin, hoping he would get my look and offer a plan for once but he was busy holding back tears as if he was scared...scared of me not choosing him this time.

His tears looked so insecure and innocent that I found it more and more hard to believe that he had betrayed me.

The air was thick with indecision and emotional tension as the situation kept on getting more and more twisted by the minute.

I couldn't think of any plan which left me with only one option...

I gripped the controls.

Mr. Dune immediately caught up with my movement, "Officer, you know it's going to be a losing game. This is simply...a foolishly desperate decision"

I looked him right in the eye as a sad smile made its way to my lips.

I repeated what he himself had told me multiple times, "No matter what you do, never fall down to your knees in front of your opponent. If needs be, fight till your last breath and watch...how the universe bows down and clears your way as a tribute to your immense dedication..."

With trembling lips, he gripped his controls with one hand while the other reached for the firearm controls, "It didn't have to end this way, Hannah..."

"I don't have much choice, sir..." I said as I mentally planned the course this helicopter had to fly.

We were directly above GG's base and not very high above, which was not at all safe. Firstly, I needed to get away from here in any direction. I couldn't win with speed. So, I had to depend on sudden turns and surprises if I wanted to have any chance at outrunning him.

The only chance at escaping - Steering of this rusty helicopter.

I wasn't liking the odds very much.

"In that case, Officer," I saw Mr. Dune's grip tighten around the firearms stick, "My hands are tied as well...Just know that...I *did not* want this to happen"

He aimed the machine gun attached to his helicopter toward our helicopter and fired. I abruptly steered the helicopter out of the way.

Mr. Dune adjusted the aim of the helicopter towards us again but not as fast as I had feared he was capable of. After all, he *was* getting old.

"We might actually stand a chance against him," I muttered...

...Just as my gaze met a literal *missile* heading straight towards us.

CHAPTER TWENTY

PLAYING DODGEBALL WITH MISSILES

I cursed loudly and smacked the controls way more harshly than I should have because of the condition of the helicopter. I barely missed the flaming explosive by a few centimetres.

"WAS THAT A FREAKING LASM?!" Soovin screamed.

"WHAT ON EARTH IS AN LASM?!" Anna screamed while regaining her balance.

"LIGHT ANTI-STRUCTURES MISSILE!" I hollered back my reply as I struggled with the rusty controls that were a nightmare for my muscles.

"TRANSLATION?" She turned to Soovin.

"THE THING THAT A BAZOOKA LAUNCHES!" He replied.

Frank shouted something but it was beyond comprehension, thanks to the duct tape.

"Uncle, on the behalf of everyone, we didn't catch a single word of whatever you said," Anna shrugged apologetically at Frank who huffed in a mixture of irritation and frustration and glared at me as if it was all my fault.

I threw my hands into the air, "WHAT? I AM NOT THE ONE TO BLAME HERE!"

Turns out, this was not an idle thing to do when piloting the wreckage of a helicopter, *especially* when another LASM is making its way toward you.

I fumbled with the controls *yet again* to keep the helicopter flying and then, once more to avoid the stupid missile.

Funny enough, Mr. Dune was having a hard time dodging the missiles as well.

His helicopter hovered near ours, "WHO IN THE DEVIL'S NAME IS FIRING LASM AT YOU LOT?!"

"AN OLD FRIEND!" I replied while glancing pointily at Soovin.

"HEY, DON'T LOOK AT ME LIKE THAT!" Soovin said.

"YOU HAVE NO RIGHT TO TELL ME WHAT THE HECK TO DO!?" I shrieked.

"HONESTLY, WHAT DID THAT SCHMUCK *TELL* YOU?!" He screamed in irritation.

"WHAT I WAS TO DARN BLIND TO SEE, YOU LITTLE SNAKE!?" I screamed with loath as I dodged another missile.

"I KNEW THIS WEASEL MEANT NO GOOD! HE IS A TRAITOR THROUGH AND THROUGH! WHY DID I EVEN GIVE THAT CASE TO YOU!?" I heard Mr. Dune scream in frustration for the first time as he dodged another missile.

"HOW DARE YOU CALL MY DAD THAT, OLD MAN!?" Anna screamed.

"ANNA, HOW DARE YOU CALL HIM AN OLD MAN!?" I thundered.

"WELL, HE IS OLD AND HE IS MAN, IS HE NOT?!" She retreated.

"HAN," Soovin said with pleading eyes that put my self-control to the test and made me almost miss dodging a missile, "WHAT DID HE TELL YOU-"

Mr. Dune cut him off aggressively, "STOP PLAYING WITH HER MIND, YOU LITTLE-"

"SHUT UP, ALL OF YOU!?" Frank's voice made everyone flinch.

I glanced at him and he had removed the handcuffs and duct tape by himself, "WE ARE GETTING *SHOT OUT OF THE SKY* AND ALL YOU GUYS WANT TO DO IS ARGUE LIKE TODDLERS!? I AM LITERALLY THE MOST PROFESSIONAL AND SENSIBLE ONE HERE!?"

Mr. Dune's jaw dropped, "YOU ARE WORKING WITH THEM, OFFICER-"

"YES, *SIR* AND WITH ALL DUE RESPECT," He screamed back with anger, "YOU CAN EASILY FIRE AT US RIGHT NOW TOO. SO, YOU DON'T HAVE THE RIGHT TO QUESTION *MY* LOYALTY. WE ALL ARE LITERALLY ON THE SAME TEAM. CAN WE JUST STOP PRETENDING OTHERWISE, WORK TOGETHER BEFORE WE GET SHOT OUT OF THE SKY AND *ACTUALLY* ACT LIKE CIA OFFICERS AND REPUTED ASSASSINS FOR GOD'S SAKE-"

Frank lost his balance as I steered the helicopter to dodge another missile, "It was not intentional, I swear to God, Frank!"

Mr. Dune said, "Officer Frank, I am going to have to arrest you as well"

Soovin threw his hands in the air aggressively, "WHAT IS WRONG WITH YOU?! YOU CALL *ME* A TRAITOR AND A CRIMINAL, WHOSE SIDE ARE *YOU* ON, OLD

MAN?!"

"I..."

Mr. Dune was at a loss of words. I had never seen him in doubt but here he was, his face brimming with uncertainty, "I know Officer Gorgin has not gone rouge without a solid reason but..."

Frank raised his hand, "Just to clarify-"

"Officer *Hannah* Gorgin," Mr. Dune amended, "I...I am bound my by duty to the nation"

He dodged another missile and aimed his firearm at us.

Dodging LASMs and the bullets of an experienced pilot like Mr. Dune was painfully hard as it was but given the condition of the helicopter we were in; it was just impossible.

"We can't do this..." I muttered.

Soovin said, "Maybe we-"

"OFFICER, BEHIND YOU!" Mr. Dune exclaimed.

Before I could look back, Soovin replied, "We are not falling for that silly outdated trick, old man, old man!"

I asked myself, *Was I really about to fall for that?*

Frank said, "No offense sir, but gosh, we expected better from you!"

"ARE YOU KIDDING ME? LOOK BEHIND, YOU IDIOTS!" He sounded so genuine this time that I had the urge to actually turn around.

"Is this guy good?" Anna asked skeptically.

"Of course!"

"Not at all!"

I and Soovin answered simultaneously.

She turned to Frank who shrugged, "Kind of"

She stared at Mr. Dune and wondered aloud, "I have so many questions"

"LOOK. BEHIND," Mr. Dune screamed louder than ever.

Anna turned around casually, "See? There is nothing- MOM, LOOK BEHIND!?"

I turned around and met an LASM aimed towards us, barely a foot away from the helicopter.

I immediately lunged at the control stick for dear life.

The impact was massive. Everybody on the helicopter was thrown into one corner or the other while my head was slammed against god knows what.

All I knew was that it hurt like hell.

I immediately glanced up at the missile we had narrowly dodged...the missile that was now headed straight toward Mr. Dune.

"NO!" I let out a gut-wrenching scream.

There was nowhere near enough time for Mr. Dune to dodge it. All he managed to do was slide the helicopter a bit further.

The missile hit the tail of the helicopter and blasted.

I watched in utter shock and horror as Mr. Dune tried to regain control of the helicopter but it was too late.

The helicopter began spinning without any sense of direction.

After trying his best and failing, Mr. Dune reached for his emergency parachute which fell out of the spinning helicopter and opened mid-air...without Mr. Dune.

I focused on his face thinking, *He must have a backup plan, some idea to save himself.*

His face showed a crude shock and then...acceptance of his fate.

"He doesn't have another parachute..." I murmured as my mind started working.

A thought came to my mind, *Could I...?*

I did some calculations in a fraction of a second involving air resistance, gravity, speed and all other possible parameters my mind could think of.

There was a 1% chance of this working out. I was getting sick of this number at this point.

"I would've tried at 0.001% too..." I said truthfully to myself.

"HAN!" Frank and Soovin exclaimed together.

Frank continued, "I know what you are thinking. IT'S A BIG NO!"

I saw Mr. Dune fall out of the helicopter as well. He was going to fall to his death unless...

"He *saved* us," I unstrapped myself hastily from the pilot's seat, "And that is *why* he is in there...I am going "

Soovin shouted, "HAN-"

But I had already jumped off the helicopter, my eyes desperately shifting from the falling parachute to Mr. Dune.

There is a 1% chance. I have got this. I can do this, I forced myself to think along these lines but all I could think was, *AAAAAHHHH! I AM AN IDIOT!*

CHAPTER TWENTY-ONE

SOOVIN LOVES PUSHING HIS LUCK

The wind was roaring past my ear while I was regretting my decision beyond limits.

Well, this was an incredibly foolish way to die after all I've been through, I thought miserably.

Still, I knew I would try my best because...I didn't want to die, duh.

I calmed my mind and locked my eyes on the parachute. I adjusted the tilt of my body and the surface area so that the wind could work the way I wanted it to.

Time was ticking and Mr. Dune was falling with more speed than I preferred. I minimized my surface area that was in contact with the air to go faster.

Then, I have no idea how but I managed to equip the parachute mid-air. It was one of my many unknown skills that I had no desire to test the presence of unless absolutely necessary.

The battle is not won, I reminded myself as I looked up to find Mr. Dune two seconds away from passing me at lightning speed.

I steered the parachute hastily and somehow managed to catch him, surprising even myself.

He was unconscious and his head was bleeding, probably due to some heavy part of the helicopter bashing his head.

I was hoping he would be conscious and we could together make some quick plan to save both our skins but now, I was left on my own.

First things first, I thought, *If things don't change, we are going to end up at GG's base AGAIN.*

I had no intention of serving Mr. Dune and myself on a silver platter to him. So, I steered away the parachute as far as possible from that wrecked place.

Now, I was heading straight for an ocean to drown in.

"Just perfect," I shouted bitterly, "Now, we are both gonna die"

"Not so fast," I heard a reply from above me.

I glanced that way and found Soovin steering the helicopter down towards us while Frank leaned out of the window to give him directions and tell me how big of an idiot I was.

He was going bonkers, "WHO IN THEIR RIGHT MIND DOES THAT?! A bit to the left, Soovin. YOU ARE IN A WORLD OF TROUBLE, HANNAH GORGIN! Lower the helicopter a bit, bud"

I was so grateful for not drowning to my death that I didn't even retaliate. Possibly because even *I* knew that was pretty idiotic and reckless.

First, an unconscious Mr. Dune, and then I was pulled inside the helicopter.

"Is there a first-aid kit in here somewhere?" I asked while removing the remains of the parachute and chucking it outside.

Frank handed me one without even stopping his rants about how he would tape me to my seat if I tried to pull any more stunts.

I blocked out his voice and concentrated on Mr. Dune.

He was bleeding a lot.

Although he was a tough guy, his age factor was making me worried. In this age and condition, he couldn't afford to lose even half of the blood he had already lost.

This was going to be a tough battle.

To distract my mind from thinking all that could go wrong, I decided to use it while working on his injury.

Frank paused for a second to catch his breath and I lunged at the opportunity, "What's the plan now?"

He replied without missing a beat, "I am thinking of GETTING YOU A BRAIN THAT YOU CAN CONSULT BEFORE LITERALLY JUMPING OFF A HELICOPTER MID-AIR-"

"Uncle, Mom is right. Where do we need to go? Also, this is not the time to blame her," Anna said.

I turned to her with affectionate eyes, "Thank god, someone actually gets-"

"We'll have plenty of time to blame her later by taking turns once we are settled somewhere safe," She completed and I scowled.

I was *not* looking forward to it.

"Well, we can't go back to my house because that goofball knows that place now," Frank said, sitting down heavily.

"He knows Mom's place too," I wondered aloud while treating Mr. Dune's head injury.

"Um..." Soovin said uncertainly from the pilot's seat, "I do have a connection that might help..."

I turned to Frank and gave him a 'Believe-me-don't-trust-him-right-now' look.

He understood but frowned in confusion as if saying 'Are you crazy? It's *Soovin*'.

My nod and begging eyes seemed to say, 'Trust me, please' and 'I'll fill you in later'.

Through uncertain and confused eyes, he smiled reassuringly meaning 'I have got your back but you better fill me in soon'.

I smiled in return. I knew he was the one person I could count on, no matter what.

"You guys do have a voice," Anna said, "Why not use it?"

"Okay, what are you both thinking?" Soovin said from the front, "I hate your little sibling codes that I can't decode"

"You don't need to," I replied coldly.

"She is really mad at you, buddy. Don't push your luck," Frank laughed it off but I knew exactly what he was trying to do.

"OKAY HAN, WHAT DID-"

"Don't. Push. Your. Luck," Cold contempt and threat were dripping from my voice and I was well aware of it.

Yet, I did nothing to disguise it in the slightest because I was way too busy controlling my urges to throw him off the helicopter.

He smacked the controls in frustration.

"Are you literally going to kill all of us because Mom is mad? Beating this already dead helicopter is not a great idea, Dad," Anna rolled her eyes at his childish behaviour which made me smile despite myself as I gave Mr. Dune's dressing some final touches.

She looked at me and muttered, "Mission Accomplished"

I leaned over and pressed a gentle kiss to her forehead only to hear Soovin mutter under his breath, "Never thought I'd be jealous of a fifteen-years-old teenage girl who is *my daughter*"

Since I couldn't kill him in front of Anna, I decided to let it go...for now, anyway.

"Where or rather *who* is your connection, bud?" Frank asked, getting us back on track.

"It's...Someone..."

More secrets. Great, I sighed deeply, *How DID I ever trust this guy?*

"It's a bit far away but we will be safe...probably," He replied with a shrug.

"How far away, precisely?" Frank asked.

He sighed out, "Norway"

"That's *really* far away, Dad," Anna said skeptically.

He shrugged once more, "It's our best bet!"

"Well, then...I say we book a hotel somewhere a bit far away for the night and then, decide what to do," Frank suggested.

"Sounds good to me," Soovin said and Anna agreed.

Frank looked at me for approval and I muttered, "Whatever"

"One problem, though," Soovin said while taking a slight turn, "Hotels generally don't allow men with one leg in the grave and a head injury like that"

I thought for a bit, "I'll take care of that"

"How exactly will you-"

"I'll take care of that," I repeated sternly.

He cursed lightly under his breath and Frank looked downright puzzled and more curious and concerned than ever.

He side-eyed me as if to say, 'You better tell me *everything*'

I took in a deep breath, *When did life become so damn twisted, again?*

"How far shall we go before looking for a hotel?" Soovin asked.

I looked outside.

The sun was melting at the horizon, washing the sky in a beautiful tinge of orange and red as a flock of birds chirped sweetly while flying away.

I thought aloud, "We would prefer to reach before it's too dark but we would also prefer to go as far away as possible. Also, the hotel should be secluded and discreet. Before going into the hotel, we would also need a disguise to be on the safer side"

"That seems like a lot to do before dark considering the sun is already setting. Time might be an issue," Soovin said and wearily rolled his shoulders.

He has not piloted a helicopter for ages...if anything I know about him IS true, I thought, *He must be tired...*

I sighed, unable to control my concern even after all that he had done and had been hiding, "Not when I am the pilot. Get up"

"Or maybe we can-"

"Time needs to be saved. Now, hurry up," I said, fully knowing that time was not the reason for my actions.

He persisted, "Han, I think-"

"Get up, man. What did I tell you about pushing your luck, ha?" Frank said.

Soovin huffed in frustration and got up unenthusiastically.

I sat down heavily on the pilot's seat and gripped the controls.

"Just remember the condition of this helicopter before you speed-"

He was cut off when I doubled the speed immediately and the helicopter shot forward while creaking loudly.

Maybe I should consider its condition, I thought as I lowered the speed a bit, *I surely don't want the helicopter to crumble into pieces mid-air. There is only one parachute and five people.*

After we were quite far away from GG's base, I lowered the height of the helicopter a bit and began scanning the view below for a shop that could help us with our disguises. A hotel near it would be too good to be true.

The stock of a theatrical company would be most suitable for the job.

The sun was beginning to disappear. It had started hiding below the horizon as the last of its glow grew weaker.

Oh come on, I groaned mentally, *Can't luck be on my side for once?*

Just as that thought occurred to me, my lingering gaze settled over a suitable shop.

I sighed softly, "Finally..."

I started lowering the helicopter while steering it towards a bit of an overgrowth near the shop. Suddenly, my wandering eyes settled on a dark and shady corner where stood a seemingly deserted hotel with a broken sign that was meant to spell 'YOU ARE GOING TO LOVE THE STAY, FRIEND' but instead read 'YOU ARE GOING TO END'.

"I am starting to think some force is watching us from heaven and purposefully making our lives a laughing stock," I heard Soovin mutter as I landed the helicopter smoothly on the soft ground.

"The shop looks pretty promising," I said as I turned off the engine.

"Let's get going, then," Frank said.

"Actually," I interrupted, "I was thinking that all of us should not go together. It will only raise suspicion. Also, if somehow either the CIA or GG's men manage to find us, it will be a lot easier for one of us to escape than our whole pack. Plus, we can't risk the helicopter or we will be stuck in the middle of nowhere"

"But one can get captured easily. It's way too risky," Soovin said.

"Two can go," Anna suggested with a shrug, "It won't put only a single person at risk and still manage the safety of the helicopter and even a quick rescue if needs be"

"I told you having her on the time was a great idea," Frank smiled.

"Who two?" I asked.

"Let's see..." Frank said, "You going seems like a good idea because you would know the best which disguises to buy"

"You and me, then. It's settled," I said while unstrapping myself from the pilot's seat.

"Excuse me? I am here too," Soovin argued but I had already anticipated this.

"We need someone who knows how to fly the helicopter to stay here," I replied while getting up.

"Frank knows it too!" He pointed out.

"No, he doesn't," I replied nonchalantly.

Frank frowned, "Han, actually I-"

I shot him a death glare and he backtracked quickly, "Yeah, I don't"

"You were the one who flew us to GG's base," Soovin scowled.

"I...forgot," Frank said, wincing at his horrible lie.

"Really, dude? You-"

"You heard him. Frank, let's go," I cut him off.

"Really, Han, how stupid do you think I am?" Soovin folded his arms.

"Oh, I know you are anything but stupid," I couldn't keep the bitterness from my voice, "Now, cut the slack and stop wasting time"

He opened his mouth to argue further but I stepped out of the helicopter before he could utter a single word and heard Frank mutter an apology before following me.

He caught up with me and asked, "Okay Han, what the hell happened?"

CHAPTER TWENTY-TWO

CALLING AN OLD FRIEND

"I am thinking we could postpone that conversation for a bit," I shrugged uncertainly.

"You are really going to leave me hanging?" He asked jokingly.

"Look Frank, the middle of a gigantic crowd is just not the best place for a conversation like this. All you should know is that..." I sighed deeply, "That guy cannot be trusted"

"Are you sure GG hasn't like...twisted your mind a bit?" He said carefully as if he was afraid of angering me somehow.

I thought for a bit and then, said, "It could be a possibility but...whatever he told me lined up perfectly with a conversation of Soovin I had accidentally overheard"

"Okay then...at least tell me the degree of trust we can show him. Like, maybe he messed up one time but is really on our side?"

I huffed, "Considering that he wanted to hand me over to crazy criminals, I would prefer not trusting him at all"

"What?" Frank looked more skeptical than ever and let out a string of curses that made even *me* flinch at the intensity.

He thought for a bit and then said, "Han, are you sure about this?"

I stopped and looked him dead in the eye, "How exactly do you think I ended up at GG's base?"

His frown cleared and he scowled, "Han, come on! Why would he hand you over to *GG?* That's plain ridiculous! GG is after *him.* They wouldn't be doing any trades!"

"I never said he was betraying me to GG. GG actually ended up ruining his plan of handing me over to his stupid mafia family...and I have no idea how to feel about that"

Frank blinked a few times, "Okay, are you going to elaborate or not because my head has started to spin?"

"Not now, Frank," I said as we continued walking towards the shop.

He muttered some pretty strong words for Soovin and said, "Remind me why are we not killing that snake yet?"

I did not have an answer to that.

All I knew was that *now* wasn't the right time. But then, will it ever be the right time for my stupid heart?

He read my face, "You seem like you could use some venting out"

I sighed out, "I still can't believe that I fell for that idiot's plan...I am also doubting if this is real-"

"Wait," Frank stopped out of the blue, "If it was all his plan and he is not on our side, then, why have we left Anna alone with that back-stabber?"

"Long story short, Anna is completely safe with him but *we* definitely are not. In fact, she is the *only* person safe with him"

"Okay, this is getting more and more twisted by the minute. When am I getting the full explanation, again?"

"Probably at the hotel we will be staying at," I shrugged, "We also need to utilize that time to think of our next move. We sure as hell won't go to his *connection in Norway* and I don't think either of us can hide the fact that we know about his plans for long. However, you need to pretend like we did not have this conversation, got it?"

"Really?"

"We can't afford to let him get suspicious, Frank. We are not ready with any plan and once we are," I flexed my fingers, "Let's just say he is going to be *really* sorry"

"But...what about Anna...? Are you planning to leave-"

"Let's worry about that once we are at the hotel and focus on the task at hand," I cut him off as we entered the shop, mainly because I had no answer to that question.

Later, I reminded myself, *Focus, Gorgin.*

We came out of the shop fifteen minutes later with a bag full of stuff and a certain blonde's wallet completely empty.

"This place was so damn expensive," Frank scowled as he smacked the door of the shop.

I just smiled while shaking my head and advanced towards the helicopter with Frank at my heels.

We decided to approach the helicopter from the side to avoid the jostling crowd present directly between us and our helicopter.

I stopped dead in my tracks and strained my ears as hushed faint whispers floated towards them.

My hand immediately reached for the hundred or so places I had hidden my guns at only for me to remember that all of them were left behind at GG's base.

Frank saw my movements and quietly handed me a spare gun while loading his.

We tip-toed towards the bush dangerously close to our helicopter, from where the hushed whispers were coming.

My shoulders relaxed a bit when I recognized Anna and Soovin's voices.

I turned to Frank and mouthed, 'What are they doing outside?'

He shrugged in response but didn't relax or speak aloud meaning that he agreed with me on eavesdropping a bit.

After all, Soovin had already shown his true colours. Who knows what else he had in store for us? Given my luck, it was better to be mentally prepared for another blow.

I heard Soovin mutter, "Han is going to kill me if she gets to know what I am doing, especially if she sees *who* I am involving in this activity..."

"Let's be honest Dad," Anna said while trying to see something far away while sitting on Soovin's shoulders, "Mom's gonna kill you either way. What did you do to make her *this* mad?"

He held up his hands defensively, "Woah. First of all, child, it's none of your business. Secondly, I am trying to figure that out myself!"

"Okay, Dad, first of all, I am *not* a child. Secondly, I know you are not the smartest but Geez! Even I didn't know you were stupid enough to not even recognize your mistakes"

"Do you see anything or not?" He asked impatiently.

"There is nothing! What *do* you expect me to see?"

"I thought she would at least tell Frank what was going on and I could get some idea of the situation but you can't even find your mother!"

"Hey, I am not the one with advanced training!"

She climbed down from Soovin's shoulder.

He said, "Let's leave it and get inside the helicopter before she comes, then"

"Don't worry, Dad," she barely resisted a smile, "You are not going to die if she doesn't talk to you, you know?"

Anna walked towards the helicopter, smirking the entire way while Soovin muttered something about stupid teenagers under his breath before following her.

Frank turned to me and whispered, "Han...are you sure Soovin...?"

The question hung in the air and I could see it swirling around in front of my eyes. Still, I had no answer to this question.

"I...I honestly have no idea what to believe and what not to believe right now Frank," I sighed wearily.

"Hey, it's fine..." He replied softly, "You are *Hannah Gorgin,* you'll figure this out"

I passed him a smile and we went inside the helicopter, acting oblivious.

Soovin immediately looked at Frank with a questioning face that I could read like the back of my hand. Frank merely shrugged and gave him a disappointing look. Soovin's shoulders slouched.

All his actions were making me reconsider everything, *Is he really innocent or just an ultra-talented actor?*

I opened the bag with all the stuff in it and laid down the items on the floor, "Quick everyone, it is almost dark. Put these over your current outfits. We need them until we are locked inside our rooms"

Within ten minutes, we all were well-disguised except one...

"What about him?" Anna pointed towards Mr. Dune.

I replied, "A mere phone call is all that is needed"

"God, I don't like the sound of that..." Frank muttered.

I took out my phone and took a deep breath, mentally preparing myself for what I was about to do, for what *needed* to be done.

My hands trembled a bit as I searched for *that* name in my contacts.

Frank looked over my shoulders and exclaimed, "OH MY GOD, HAN! You can't-it's gonna-why the hell are you-?"

"Sorry, I didn't realize you had a *better*, *masterfully* laid out plan, Frank!" I retorted.

"Han...It will complicate things...This is *the last thing* we need right now"

"Frank...we need to. No matter what you say...he *deserves* to know, " was all I said as I pressed the call button.

"No, no, no, no, no," Frank kept on muttering and pacing as the bell rang while Soovin and Anna gave us weird looks.

My heartbeat increased with every little ring of my phone as a million questions flooded my mind. I had begun second-guessing this decision as well and had almost ended the call but before I could, the buzzing stopped.

A faint gasp met my ears as I heard a familiar whisper of disbelief from the other side of the line, "Hannah...?"

I took a deep breath that did little to calm my nerves.

My voice trembled slightly as I said, "Be quick...Please...Your father is fighting for his last breath"

CHAPTER TWENTY-THREE

ERUPTION OF EMOTIONS

"Han, why are you-" He seemed at a loss of words but being the brave man he has always been, he gathered himself within a fraction of a second and all I could hear was a shuddering breath.

He has realized why, I couldn't help but think.

I could hear the tears in his voice when he said, "Where...?"

Although he couldn't see me, I smiled faintly, "You already know that...don't you, Wade?"

After a moment of silence, he replied, "I am coming, Han but..."

I heard his sad hollow laugh that made me flinch with concern and my eyes water, "...Did you really need something like this to happen before calling me after all these years...?"

I had no reply to that, just grieving and tearful silence.

I managed to whisper faintly while choking on tears, "I had promised him to never contact you, Wade...But...Don't waste time...Please, come fast...for me, Wade"

I could feel the heat radiating off Soovin and it was getting increasingly difficult to ignore it.

"I am on my way, Han...Just remember...If you need anything, I'll always be there...And I am doing this only for you...*not for him,* " He said as his voice trembled, with bitter rage or tender emotions, I couldn't tell.

I gulped and cut the call.

"This is *so so so* messed up," Frank said while rubbing his temples, "We have literally ensured our doom, Han...GG...Wade...He is GG's dad when it comes to mafia and crime...Why did you...We are all gonna *die, Han!"*

"Who the hell *was* that guy?" Soovin gritted out through a clenched jaw.

"Two things," I looked him coldly in the eye, "One, it's none of your business, and two, we don't have time to waste. It's already dark. You better get a grip on yourself"

He clenched his fists and turned to Frank, "Who *was* that guy?"

Frank sighed, "Buddy, trust me, you *really* don't want to know"

"Maybe I do!" He bit back.

I sighed with boredom, "Well...Wade is a man of his word. Knowing him, he'll be here in fifteen minutes at most. I suggest we get moving"

"Knowing him? How *do* you know that 'man of his word' ?" Soovin demanded again, only for me to ignore him completely...yet again.

I wondered, *How is he still trying to talk? Doesn't he get the hint?*

I was in no mood to explain anything to him and more importantly, I felt that I didn't owe any explanation to him of all people.

"I mean it, Frank...You *know* how ugly it will get if they both cross paths," I said.

Frank shuddered from head to toe and whispered to himself, "From what I know...He wouldn't hurt you but...he will destroy anyone who lays a finger on you...That includes GG...If they clash...It will be worse than a World War..."

He knew exactly what I was talking about. We were walking on cold, thin ice that could break anytime and send us straight to hell.

If GG and Wade crossed paths...Not only will the world of crime go up in flames, but every single person who stands in their way will crumble to dust.

It would be a disaster for mankind.

Frank got up immediately, "No time for any discussions. Let's get to the hotel as quickly as we can or...Man, I don't even want to think about it"

"Anna," I said softly, "Come on, let's go"

She looked at me and asked, "Mom, was that this guy's son?"

I looked towards where she was pointing to find Mr. Dune and replied, "Yeah"

"How bad will it be if they *do* cross paths?" She asked sincerely.

I sighed, "You want the bitter truth or a comforting lie?"

"The truth," She replied without any hesitation.

I kneeled down so that I was at eye level with her sitting silhouette and placed my hand over her shoulder, "Imagine...what would happen if...let's say we all were locked in a big room, unarmed...with GG and his thousand or so men, armed to the teeth..."

She gulped nervously, "We all will die the most...painful and horrible death...?"

"Right," I smiled at her encouragingly and then said as honestly as I could, "Now multiply that by ten. *That* is what would happen if Wade finds us here and gets to know about GG. I *mean it,* Anna"

She turned to Soovin and said shrilly, her voice filled with fear and urgency, "Dad, I *really* think we should get going"

We all got out of the helicopter and started jogging towards the old and broken hotel.

Suddenly, Anna stopped, "Uncle, can you tie my shoelace please?"

Frank looked puzzled but replied, "Um...Sure...? You lot keep moving"

I continued walking and Soovin caught up with me. Only then did I realize why and what Anna had done. I felt like facepalming myself.

"Han, who is Wade?" He asked as soon as we were walking together.

"I told you back there, didn't I?" I replied sharply and increased my speed.

"Why was he calling you 'Han'?" He pressed.

His voice portrayed anger...and something else as well that I was too riled up to decipher.

"Maybe because that's my name, genius?" I scowled irritatedly, hoping he would leave me alone.

"That is *not* your name. That's a nickname-"

That was it.

I stopped and turned to face him, "After all you have done, what gives you *the audacity* to argue with me?!"

"What have I...What didGavin tell you, Han!?" He lost it as well.

"WHAT *YOU* SHOULD HAVE!?" I yelled.

We both were basically screaming in the middle of the deserted road now.

He was taken aback by my sudden rage and tried for a calm approach, "Tell me your side of the story, Han and I'll tell you mine...please"

"Wow. You are a damn good actor"

"TELL ME, HAN!?"

"FINE, THEN!"

Unable to stop myself, I grabbed him by the collar and leaned closer to him so that we were mere inches apart.

Staring right into his soul, I gritted out, "Look me in the eye and tell me you have no idea what he told me or rather...what you failed to tell mein *five bloody years,* Soovin"

His earlier angry face flickered and all I could see was...guilt. That was all the confirmation I needed. He *had* betrayed me. His face was an open testimony to this.

I continued as a wave of emotions hit me, "You *betrayed* me...Given your history, I should've known better for a CIA Officer but...Please tell me at least a part of it was real..."

He shook his head and said frantically, "Han...I know I have made mistakes but...I never...All I did was not tell the entire truth. I didn't think you would feel *this* betrayed!"

Tears filled my eyes as I said, *"You didn't think I would feel this betrayed?!* Be honest for once in your entire life and tell me did any of this even mean anything to you...? Did *I* ever mean *anything* to you...?"

He shook his head while saying through tear-filled eyes, "You mean a lot to me, Han. It was *needed.* I never *wanted* to do that to them"

"Who 'them' ?" I pushed him away in irritation, "All I know and care about is that everything for five years was a mere act for one of your bloody plots and you were ready

to *trade* me, *you rascal!"*

A frown appeared on his forehead, "Trade you? What are you talking about? *How could you even think that way?"*

"Great! Now, you are going to pretend like you didn't even do anything!" I grabbed his collar once again and had the urge to tear him apart for all that he had done.

My heart was beating out of my chest and I could feel his frantic heartbeat as well.

His eyes held my fiery gaze, "Han, I feel like there is a misunderstanding-"

He froze and his eyes widened in realization, "Oh no...he has fed you a manipulated story. Han, believe me, I-"

"Believe you? How can *anyone* believe you when all you have *ever* done is betray every hand that made the foolish decision to trust you!"

I could see the hurt and anger in his emerald green eyes that my words had caused but I was too out of control to care anymore.

He shouted, "SHUT UP! YOU DON'T KNOW *ANYTHING* THAT HAPPENED!"

"OH WELL, CAN YOU GUESS *WHY?* BECAUSE YOU ARE TOO BIG OF A COWARD TO TELL ANYONE ANYTHING WITH YOUR OWN BLOODY MOUTH!?"

I am pretty sure that if this had continued any further, neither GG nor Wade was needed for our doom because we both would have torn each other apart right there and then.

"GET OFF EACH OTHER!?" I heard Frank and Anna scream at us but neither of us even diverted our gaze from the other.

Frank rushed to my side and Anna to Soovin's. They both pulled us apart before we could kill each other with our murderous gazes, and hands if necessary.

The flame between us had turned into a fire that was burning both of us...slowly, painfully, and then, all at once.

Frank finally managed to drag me further towards the hotel while Anna and Soovin followed closely behind but far enough so that neither I nor Soovin could get our hands on each other.

"Han, what happened?" Frank asked.

I gritted out, "I am *so sick* of that phrase"

He judged my mood and luckily for him, decided not to probe me further.

Ten minutes later, we were all at the weathered and broken building of the hotel that seemed a second away from crumbling to dust. Frank and Anna were standing between Soovin and me at the reception because they knew we would strangle each other if we got the chance.

The voice of an old lady came from the interior, "The cinema is two blocks down to the right!"

"Um, we need accommodation...?" Frank said into thin air.

"I beg your pardon?" The lady seemed baffled.

Frank sighed and repeated.

The lady immediately came out and stood at the reception.

"Hi, can we get a room for four?" Frank asked the old receptionist who looked seconds away from leaving this Earth.

He glanced at Anna and then, they both glanced at Soovin and me looking daggers at each other.

"On second thought," Frank told the receptionist, "Four different rooms near each other, please"

"Sir, only two rooms are available at the moment. However, each of them does have two separate beds," The old lady told him.

Anna looked skeptical, "Are you seriously telling us that people *come here?*"

She spun around slowly, highlighting the condition of the hotel.

The old receptionist narrowed her eyes at her.

Trying to protect the non-existent dignity of the old building with hollow claims that one can spot from a mile away, she said pointedly, "The rooms are being *repaired,* you spoilt child"

Anna scowled at her, "Don't you *dare* call me that, you old little-"

"We will take those two rooms, please!" Frank interrupted.

"The duration of the stay?" She asked.

"One night, till now," He added with a meaningful look, "But we *might* prolong it depending on how reasonable your price is"

"$100"

He scowled, "Are you kidding me? *$100 for this?*"

"The prices are fixed. Take it or leave it," her experienced eyes knew we were desperate.

Frank turned to us and whispered so that old lady with not-so-sharp hearing could not hear, "Please tell me you guys have some cash or we will have to sleep on the road"

CHAPTER TWENTY-FOUR

SOOVIN BREAKS DOWN

"I do," Soovin and I replied at the same time and our glaring contest began again as if it had never stopped.

"One of you will be fine," Anna shrugged.

How immature do you think we are...? We *definitely did not* fight over paying. Not at all...

We did.

"Stop, both of you!" Frank exclaimed, "Soovin, $50 and Han, $50...Anna is more mature than both of you *combined*"

We both scowled in irritation and slammed $50 each at the reception table.

The old lady peered over her foggy spectacles at our behaviour and muttered, "Interesting..."

Anna snapped her fingers in front of her, "Keys"

The receptionist clenched her jaw at the tone but bit her tongue as she counted the money and then handed over the keys to Frank while explaining the location of the rooms.

Frank tossed one to Anna and nodded at her, "You and Soovin. I and Hannah"

"Do we even have any other option?" She said as she dragged Soovin away.

"Smart girl," Frank muttered as he turned to me, "Come on, Han. I don't know about you but I am ready to drop dead and wake up after 50 good hours of sleep"

"We both know we need to leave early in the morning, Frank. Fooling Wade is not a piece of cake and you very well know it"

"Do you *really* need to bring this up again and again? I am already in full panic mode, Han! How do you expect me to sleep? I swear to God if I get nightmares including Wade, I will wake you up at 3 in the morning!"

I smiled and started climbing the stairs, "Come on, blondie! Or do you want Wade to come and carry you up the stairs?"

Shaking his head, he followed me, "Continue bothering me like this and I will tell Mom-"

He stopped abruptly as the playful atmosphere vanished.

I felt as if a cold metal rod was poking at my heart. *Mom. How could have I forgotten about her for this long...?*

"I mean...Let's just get to the room," He frantically tried to change the topic.

"Frank...Did you get any update on her while I was away...?" I said, judging his body language.

"Han...Let's just...Let's just get to the room and sleep for now," Frank was basically running up the stairs at this point.

I caught up with him and grabbed his shoulder, "Frank, *how is mom?*"

"Han, let's just take some rest and...we'll talk about this tomorrow..."

"You very well know I am not letting this go, Frank. HOW *IS* MOM?"

"Look...Her condition is not the best," I could see beads of sweat covering his forehead.

His hands trembled slightly, a little less than his voice as he opened the door to our room, "She...she will get better soon, though"

"Frank...are you good...?"

"Yeah, of course-I..." He gulped hard as he finally turned around to face me, "It's just...When you both were in coma...and neither of you was showing any signs of recovery...That was a pretty *horrible* time, Han and then GG took you away...Let's just say I had to deal with a lot of mental pressure"

A tear trickled down his cheek.

Maybe *he* was the one who could use some venting out.

I reached towards him and hugged him tightly, "It's fine...I am here and soon...so will she..."

I felt his body relax and heard his shuddering breath as if he was finally letting go of the weight he had been carrying for so long.

After a moment, he pulled away and wiped his eyelids, "Yeah...Of course..."

Something felt odd about his voice and behaviour when he repeated, "Of course...she will"

"Is there something else you want to tell me?" I pressed him gently.

"No..." he smiled at me weakly.

"Frank, are you sure because your condition-"

There was a knock on the open door.

I turned around to find the old receptionist standing there.

"Yes?" I asked.

"The room right next to yours is the kitchen with the pantry included. As it is 9 PM now, if you need anything to eat before 8 AM, feel free to use it and the materials within it. I am the only one here and I am going home now"

"What on earth are you taking $100 for, then?" Frank grimaced.

She raised her eyebrows, "You seem to be unfamiliar with this area, sir. All I will say is that you should be grateful we are not charging you for the materials you use from the pantry"

Frank grumbled, "Oh really? I don't-"

I stepped in between them and offered the lady a smile, "Thanks a lot for the information. Now, we won't delay your activities any further"

She smiled at me approvingly and went on her way, closing the door behind her.

"Han, why did you stop me?" Frank complained.

"You really think she was worth it? Also, come to think of it, *will* we eat anything before 8 AM? I don't think so. You just said you were ready to sleep for 50 hours straight. I am damn sure you won't even be up before 8 AM"

He chuckled, "You know me way too much"

Suddenly I heard a scream from the adjacent room...where Soovin and Anna were staying.

"DAD, YOU NEED TO STOP BLAMING YOURSELF!?" Anna was screaming.

Soovin's angry scream was laced with frustration and emotional vulnerability, "YOU DON'T GET IT, ANNA! NO MATTER WHAT I TRY TO DO...I JUST HURT PEOPLE. THAT'S ALL I AM GOOD AT!"

"COME ON, DAD! YOU CAN'T BE SERIOUS!?"

I felt a pang of guilt in my chest.

Soovin *hated* being anything other than strong in front of Anna. He would always prefer handling his problems alone...or with me.

This time, because his problem was *with* me, he was left alone...with no idea how to gather himself...I was the one who guided him through that every time.

I bit my lip, unsure of everything for the billionth time.

His puzzled look when I had said that he was ready to trade me resurfaced in my mind.

The way he was begging me to listen to him at least once. I had avoided it because I knew that if he was clever enough to lay out such a realistic act for five years, he was surely clever enough to cook up something at a moment's notice to defy GG's claims, no matter if they were true or not.

If I was sure of something, it was that he had the potential to make me believe anything. He knew me too well and too much. All my soft spots as well as my weaknesses lay bare in front of him, leaving me completely exposed and vulnerable.

But then...what if he was indeed telling the truth...?

GG was the sort of guy to mentally twist someone enough for them to believe anything. He had no code of ethics anyhow and could be lying about the whole thing.

But the phone call I heard...

"My head is going to explode," I grumbled while rubbing my temples.

"Want some coffee?" Frank offered me a smile.

"I think I'd rather sleep," I replied as a yawn escaped my mouth, "I'll wake up early and wake *you* up early to give you all the justifications you want...Maybe I'll be able to process my own thoughts by that time..."

"I feel like lying on the floor and throwing a massive tantrum until you tell me everything but God, you could do with some rest..."

I chuckled, "Glad you understand, little one but let's be honest, none of us will fall asleep before 11 PM even if we spent those two hours lying on the bed, staring into space"

"Bold of you to assume I can fall asleep by 11 PM," He smiled, "But I am going to bed, anyway!"

I went to my bed which was in front of Frank's bed and laid down heavily.

For a moment, I was reminded of my childhood.

The way mom would tuck us both in after showering us with love and affection...

Mom.

I had hit a sore spot once again.

Frank had said that she was still in a coma. I had slipped into a coma after her and had woken up what felt like ages ago.

Why had *she* not woken up yet...?

Another suspicion crept into my mind.

Frank seemed devastatingly upset at the mention of Mom. The time when we both were in coma must have been extremely hard for him but the CIA side of my brain told me there was something more to it. Was he hiding something?

Why are you doubting everyone around you? Being so paranoid is not good, especially when you need people to get out of this muck you are stuck in, My mind seemed to say.

It was probably right.

Maybe I was overthinking or didn't remember it correctly?

I heard Frank shift in his bed.

"Lost in the labyrinth of your mind as well?" I asked with a hollow laugh.

I heard him chuckle lightly, "Yeah"

"Wanna unload some of your worries on me?" I smiled even though he couldn't see me in the pitch-dark lighting of the room.

He sighed and said in a grim tone, "I was just thinking that...Han, calling Wade was an incredibly big mistake. What makes you think he will save Mr. Dune?"

"I know they never got along but-"

"That's a bit of an understatement, Han. They have always been ready to *kill each other*-"

"He is still his son, Frank...He might not have chosen to follow Mr. Dune's footprints but...he still has his blood in him"

"Blood doesn't make family. We both know that. What if he is still sore about everything?"

"Mr. Dune or Wade?"

"Man, I don't even know anymore," He sighed.

I replied in a similar tone, "Knowing both of them, neither would have forgiven the other. They are both absurdly unforgiving people"

"Then, why did you call him?"

"Well, it *is* true that unforgiveness runs in their blood but...Believe me, Wade *will* save Mr. Dune, especially after..."

I stopped mid-sentence as the events of that night revolved in front of my eyes. I tried to divert my mind but it was too late.

Wade screaming with his CIA uniform stained with blood, "Dad is going to kill me!"...I trying to reassure him...Wade holding a gun to my head...Wade screaming, "YOU NEVER EVEN TRIED TO UNDERSTAND ME!"...Mr. Dune screaming, "YOU ARE NO SON OF MINE!"...Wade saying through tear-filled eyes, "He has left me with no other choice"...Thousands of police sirens wailing...Mr. Dune collapsing on the floor...Martin lying on the hospital bed with a bullet shot right at his heart...

"After what, Han...?" Frank pressed.

I shivered, trying to come back to reality but my mind had already gone back to the night of 12th December and was reliving that horrific night once again. I could see all of it happening on my eyelids as I tried to block out the horrible flashback, all in vain.

Wade sobbing, "I am so sorry Han"...I screaming, "GET YOURSELF TOGETHER, WADE! THERE MUST BE ANOTHER WAY!"...Wade whispering in my ear, "Promise me, Han"...Me whispering faintly with trembling lips, "I promise, Wade"...Mr. Dune using my name for the first time, "Promise me, Hannah"...Me once again saying while holding back my tears, "I promise, sir"...Wade's message on my mobile's screen, 'For what you did for me, Han, just one call and I will burn the world down for you. Don't forget that. Anytime. I will help you no matter what happens...the same way you did for me'...A bullet piercing my shoulder as I screamed, "WADE!"

I jerked back to reality. My heart was beating faster than ever as a single tear trickled down my right cheek.

Then, as if reading my silence and hearing my laboured breathing, Frank asked, "Han...What *happened* on 12th December...?"

THE NIGHT OF 12TH DECEMBER

I was standing in the hospital, leaning over a dead body and mentally jotting down the points regarding the man who had died.

"It is definitely a murder," I muttered to myself and then turned to the doctor standing on my right side, "Where is the report-?"

Suddenly, my phone rang.

I excused myself and took out my phone from my pocket.

"Wade...?" I read the name flashing on my screen as my mind did its work, He should be on a mission with Martin. I still have no idea why Mr. Dune assigned them a joint mission. It is no secret that they both loath each other. God knows what they are up to right now...

I picked up the phone, "Wade, I am in the middle of something-"

"HAN!" His voice was laced with panic and urgency.

"What happened?" I asked, immediately concerned, "Are you fine?"

"HE...I...BULLET. HAN, COME TO BROOKLYN HOSPITAL RIGHT NOW!"

"I AM THERE ONLY! WHAT HAPPENED, WADE?"

"HAN!"

I turned around and my jaw dropped at the sight that met my eyes.

Every inch of Wade's CIA uniform was stained with blood. His blue eyes portrayed fear and guilt. His red hair was terribly messed up. His already pale, oval face was drained of every bit of colour and was white with fear.

With his trembling hands, he was holding a wheeled stretcher and on it was laying...

I cursed loudly as I and numerous doctors rushed towards Martin who was lying unconscious on the wheeled stretcher, bleeding at an alarming rate.

The first thing I noticed was a fresh bullet injury...right at his heart.

"WADE, HOW DID THIS HAPPEN?!" I screamed as I examined Martin.

He was breathing but his pulse was faint.

Wade was spitting out incoherent strings of words in panic.

"ICU, NOW!" One of the doctors screamed and they took Martin away to the ICU.

I grabbed Wade by his shoulders, "CALM DOWN, WADE! GATHER YOURSELF!"

His chest was heaving up and down rapidly. I grabbed a water bottle from the side table and offered it to him.

After a couple of deep breaths, he panted, "I was shooting at...the criminal we were after...He jumped...in front of me...I couldn't...I had already pressed the trigger...The bullet..."

"It's fine, Wade. It's absolutely fine," I tried my best to calm him down even though my own heartbeat was skyrocketing.

"Han, I...I swear I didn't mean to...It just," He frantically tried to explain.

"I know, Wade. I believe you," I told him while rubbing his back.

"DAD IS GOING TO KILL ME!" He screamed.

"No, he won't!" I tried to reassure him, "It was an accident, Wade"

"YOU REALLY THINK HE WILL BELIEVE THAT? HE WILL THINK I SHOT HIM BECAUSE OF OUR STUPID RIVILARY!" He gripped his hair, "Oh god, what do I do? What do I do? WHAT DO I DO?!"

"Mr. Dune will understand. He is your father, Wade. Now, we need to inform the headquarters-"

"NO! HAN, NO ONE WILL BELIEVE ME! I DIDN'T MEAN IT!"

"YOU ARE OVERTHINKING, WADE! And if we don't inform the headquarters that will just make matters worse! They will see it as evidence against you!"

"They don't need to know! Not now!"

"Do you really think they wouldn't find this out in seconds through CCTV of the road you-"

Suddenly, my handheld transceiver buzzed.

Mr. Dune's urgent voice came, "BROADCASTING, ALL AGENTS. OFFICER WADE HAS SHOT OFFICER MARTIN. I REPEAT OFFICER WADE HAS SHOT OFFICER MARTIN. HE IS SUSPECTED TO BE IN BROOKLYN HOSPITAL. ALL AGENTS, REACH THERE IMMEDIATELY. APPROACH WITH CAUTION AND..."

Mr. Dune's voice flickered with emotions, "SHOOT OFFICER WADE IF NEEDED. I REPEAT, YOU HAVE THE PERMIT TO SHOOT OFFICER WADE IF HE REFUSES COOPERATION. BROOKLYN HOSPITAL. EVERYONE REACH THERE, NOW!"

It beeped and the voice died.

"SEE? I TOLD YOU HE WOULD NOT BELIEVE ME. HE NEVER DID!" Wade got up.

"I'LL TALK TO HIM WADE. HE JUST...GAVE THE ORDERS HURRIEDLY!"

"HURRIEDLY?! HE JUST ORDERED ALL THE OFFICERS TO SHOOT ME, HAN!"

He suddenly stepped away from me in fear.

"I AM NOT GOING TO SHOOT YOU, YOU MORON!" I exclaimed.

"THOSE ARE YOUR ORDERS!" He screamed and took another step back.

I took out my gun and threw it away, signalling that I would not shoot him and reached towards him.

I placed my hands firmly on his shoulders and said in a soft and calm voice, "I am not going to shoot you, Wade"

A tear trickled down his cheek, "Han, I...I don't know what to do! They'll...They'll shoot me, Han!"

"No one will touch you, Wade. I am here. I'll protect you. You are safe," I tried comforting him so that he would think clearly.

He looked into my eyes and said, "You believe me, right?"

"Of course, I do, Wade! I have known you my entire life. All we need to do is tell Mr. Dune that it was all an accident and-"

"Officer Hannah Gorgin," Mr. Dune's voice came from my handheld transceiver, "You are at the Brooklyn hospital I believe"

Wade's eyes widened and he attempted to run away but I held him firmly and securely.

"Yes, sir," I replied, "Sir, Officer Wade-"

"I believe you heard my orders?"

"Yes, sir, but-"

"ARREST HIM, OFFICER. THAT'S A DIRECT ORDER FROM ME"

"BUT, SIR-"

"AM I CLEAR, OFFICER GORGIN?!"

I didn't reply. I and Wade shared a look. His face was laced with fear but I managed to combat it with friendliness and care.

"Officer..." Mr. Dune's voice softened a bit, "I know you two are close. He will come to you for help. He might try to deceive you with falsehoods"

"But sir, what if he is actually-"

Mr. Dune continued without giving an ear to me, "I knew I shouldn't have trusted him to go on the mission with Officer Martin. He was never capable of controlling himself...Officer, shoot him at sight. Don't listen to him at all and I would NOT be hearing anything other than 'Yes, sir' from you"

I looked into Wade's eyes and saw him shatter on the spot.

I knew this was a weak spot for him. He and Mr. Dune never had a healthy relationship because he had never been enough for Mr. Dune and he resented it beyond limits. Now, Mr. Dune had given the order to shoot him at sight...that too to me...

"Yes, sir," I said in a dejected tone.

Mr. Dune was going crazy. He was not going to listen to anyone right now.

"Is...is he with you, Officer...?"

Wade looked at me and his desperate eyes asked a silent question. He needed help and he could rely on no one other than me.

"No, sir," I replied confidently.

Mr. Dune sighed, "Find him and remember...Shoot him at sight"

"Yes, sir..."

The receiver went dead and Wade looked at me, "I need to run away, far away from here. I am so sorry, Han"

I screamed, "GET YOURSELF TOGETHER, WADE! THERE MUST BE ANOTHER WAY!"

My receiver beeped once again, "BROADCASTING. ALL OFFICERS, SHOOT OFFICER WADE AT SIGHT. I REPEAT, SHOOT OFFICER WADE AT SIGHT"

"He has left me with no other choice, Han..." He whispered as a tear rolled down his cheek.

I approached him with caution, "Wade, we can make it all right. We just need to-"

"Are you on my side or not?" He asked, taking a step away from me.

"Wade, I-"

"YES OR NO, HAN?"

I opened my mouth to talk some sense into him but at that exact moment, multiple sirens wailed.

Wade said to himself, "I need to go before it's too late..."

He ran towards the exit door on the backside of the hospital and I chased him all the way there.

Then, he abruptly stopped in the hallway right before the exit door. I almost bumped into him.

"Wade, stop. It's-"

"Dad is standing there, Han," He said desperately.

The sound of numerous footsteps filled the room. The Officers were coming.

"They will be here in a minute. They have shoot-at-sight orders, Han! They will not give me a chance to explain myself. We both know that!"

I remained silent because I knew what he was saying was true. This was an extremely twisted and dangerous situation.

"I..." He broke into tears, "I don't want to die, Han..."

I gulped as I took a deep breath to calm my nerves and clear my head.

If I followed my duty, Wade would die in vain. If I didn't, the officers approaching us would kill him and even if they didn't, Mr. Dune will.

His orders had made it pretty clear and he had always preferred duty over emotions. He wouldn't hesitate before killing his own son if he thought his duty demanded it.

But I couldn't let Wade die like this...

"Wade, point your gun at me," I said.

He looked up, "Han, what do you...? I am NOT using you as a shield to get out of here, Han!"

I took out his gun from his pouch and placed it in his hands.

I looked him in the eyes and said, "You have to, Wade...There is no other option...I am not letting you die like this on my watch"

He gulped and pointed his gun at me with trembling hands.

My voice quivered as I told him, "Be brave, Wade"

He took a deep breath and then, dashed towards the door which Mr. Dune was guarding while holding me as a hostage.

"WADE!" Mr. Dune screamed and pointed his gun at him, "LEAVE HER"

Wade replied in a shaky voice, "I did not want to do this, Dad"

"YOU KILLED AN OFFICER, WADE! YOU ARE NOT FIT TO WEAR THAT BADGE BECAUSE YOU CAN NOT CONTROL YOURSELF!"

"I DID NOT!"

"YOU HAD ALWAYS BEEN AN UNRELIABLE, UNTRUSTWORTHY AND AN INCOMPETENT CHILD!" Mr. Dune spoke as if he was spitting out poison.

"YOU NEVER EVEN TRIED TO UNDERSTAND ME!" He screamed back while choking on tears, "DAD-"

"YOU ARE NO SON OF MINE!" Mr. Dune thundered, "MY SON WOULDN'T KILL AN OFFICER AND THEN USE

ANOTHER OFFICER AS A HUMAN SHIELD TO SAVE HIS OWN SKIN!?"

"MAYBE BECAUSE YOU NEVER TREATED ME LIKE A SON! I DID EVERYTHING I COULD BUT I WAS NEVER ENOUGH FOR YOU!?" He screamed, "Back off, Dad...or I will shoot"

I felt his grip tighten on the gun.

Mr. Dune's eyes darted from Wade to me, assessing the situation. Then, he slowly backed away from the door.

Wade whispered in my ear so that only I could hear, "Han, promise me that you will delete every single trace that could tell Dad that you helped me and you will NOT try to convince him of my innocence at all because that will just shift all the suspicion to you. He is never going to look past his duty. You are the only one who believed me, Han. I won't stand anyone labelling you a criminal the way they labelled me one"

"Wade, I-"

"Promise me, Han," He said as more desperate tears rolled down his cheek.

I whispered faintly with trembling lips, "I promise, Wade"

A hundred Officers filtered into the room with their guns pointed at Wade and me.

We both knew what they were about to do.

"Wade, shoot my shoulder and run away," I whispered urgently.

"No, Han, I-"

"If you don't shoot my shoulder, they will shoot your head and possibly mine too. I will say your name and pretend to be betrayed. Take my car keys from my pant pocket. Please, Wade...Shoot me and run"

"I..." He took in a deep breath and fished the keys from my pocket half-heartedly, "I'll contact you as soon as I am away, Han...I will never be able to repay you for this..."

"Just go, Wade!"

Then, he pushed me and opened the door.

A bullet pierced my shoulder as I screamed, "WADE!"

As soon as I was out of the range, Mr. Dune screamed, "FIRE! CATCH HIM!"

Some Officers took me aside and tended to my shoulder as the others rushed outside.

"Officer Gorgin, are you fine?" Mr. Dune asked.

"Yes, sir," I replied, keeping my promise to Wade of not telling him anything.

The Officers returned, "Sorry sir, but he has escaped"

Mr. Dune took in a shaky breath, "Wade...how could you...?"

Suddenly, he collapsed on the floor as everyone rushed to help him.

Mr. Dune was taken to the ICU by everyone.

I waited outside the ICU for him once my bullet wound was taken care of. The entire atmosphere was engulfed by a pin-drop silence similar to the silence after a storm.

My phone buzzed.

Wade had sent me a message reading, 'For what you did for me, Han, just one call and I will burn the world down for you. Don't forget that. Anytime. I will help you no matter what happens...the same way you did for me'

Before I could type a reply, a nurse tapped on my shoulder, "The patient wishes to see you"

"Mr. Dune?" I asked.

"I believe so," She showed me the way.

Mr. Dune was lying on the bed with a dozen equipments attached to him.

He looked at me with guilt-filled eyes and said, "I am incredibly sorry for what happened, Officer Gorgin"

"It's alright, sir. Are you fine?"

He waved his hand at me, dismissing my question, "I...I never imagined Wade would do something like this. I understand that it is hard for you too"

Unsure of what to do, I nodded in reply.

"You did not deserve what you went through, Officer Gorgin"

I bit my tongue from screaming, 'NEITHER DID WADE!'

"But...I am incredibly sorry to tell you that an enquiry will be done on you-"

"An enquiry on me?" My eyebrows were probably touching the sky.

"Officer, I know you are innocent but...Higher authorities will no longer consider my word of any value after my son...I am helpless, Officer"

I bit my tongue extra hard to suppress the urge to spit out a string of terrible curses for the wrecked and messed up system.

"But my morals don't allow you to suffer because of my incompetent son"

That was the first time I felt like punching Mr. Dune in the face. After everything Wade had achieved in his career, he was calling him incompetent.

I clenched my fists to control my bubbling rage.

"The main reason for today's unfortunate events was that...Today, on 12th December, Wade's bullet gave an innocent Officer Martin the gift of death...and I will return the favour in any way before my last breath. Give me a vague hint of one of those lines, Officer, and I will help you no matter what. I can't hold back the enquiry. This is the least I can do to ensure justice"

The rebellious part of me wanted to ask, 'What about justice for Wade...? What had he done to have his entire life snatched from him in one night...?'

Instead of saying any of this, I saluted him and promised myself never to use this favour unless the circumstances absolutely called for it.

"But promise me something, Officer...Because of what he has done, you will never contact him unless necessary to save a life"

"But, sir-"

He whispered through filmy eyes that were the only proof showing that maybe he did love Wade, "He willingly ran away from everything...Promise me, Hannah"

I was so shocked that he had called me by my name that I found myself whispering with trembling lips just as I had done a few minutes ago for Wade, "I promise, sir"

A few months later, the headquarters were notified of a new mafia leader rising to the top, a guy called Wade. Over time, he became one of the most feared criminals.

Still, I couldn't bring myself to take any case related to him even when he had joined the Mafia out of spite for his father because...if I was in his place...wouldn't have I done the same...?

Yet, a single line kept me awake for days...

"The bullet on 12th December gave an innocent the gift of death, and I will return the favour in any way before my last breath"

CHAPTER TWENTY-SIX

THE 3 AM BAKERY

I jerked awake for the hundredth time as another set of flashbacks woke me up. I looked at my wristwatch. It was almost 3 AM.

I thought, *If I couldn't sleep in 5 hours, there is no way I am falling asleep now.*

And just like that, I let my thoughts take the control of my mind.

I felt like a volleyball bouncing from Soovin to Mom to Wade and then, Soovin again.

"If things continue this way, I am going to go crazy in no time," I muttered as I sat upright, any chance of me falling asleep fading into nothingness.

A thought occurred to my mind and without second-guessing it in the slightest, because I had given all the control to my thoughts, I stepped out of the room and went into the Pantry.

I let my mind wander as my hands worked on their own.

Suddenly, I heard a familiar deep voice, "Why are you baking cookies at 3 AM, Han?"

I turned around and my shoulders relaxed on seeing Frank, "I just felt like eating cookies."

He raised his eyebrows, "At 3 AM?"

"I've learned not to question how my mind works"

"You never sleep, do you?"

"I could ask the same question"

"You expected me to sleep and have sweet dreams after that story you told me?"

I chuckled while working on my cookies, "The blame is on me then, I suppose?"

"Not really because now," He jumped and sat on the kitchen counter, "We can use all this time to listen to another due story"

I sighed, "We need to, don't we?"

"Well, spit it out!"

"So...First things first, I had accidentally overheard a conversation between Soovin and someone. He was saying..."

I narrated everything with as much detail as possible up to the heated argument we had on the road outside the hotel, including the details of my *heart-warming* stay at GG's base.

He murmured, "Man, that's *so* messed up..."

"I mean...I think that's what happened but I am not sure..."

I heard some noise from behind one of the curtains and my hand immediately went to my gun.

"Relax, Han. It's probably just a cat on the outside of the window or something," Frank rolled his eyes at me, "It's 3 AM for god's sake..."

"Or this ancient hotel is finally ready to collapse," I joked and turned to baking the cookies again.

"But, how are you not sure if it all happened to you...?" Frank frowned.

"I...don't know, Frank. I think I am going crazy with all this"

"Han," He got up from the counter, "How have you not noticed this?"

"Noticed what?"

He sighed, "Typical me, have to save the day with my outside-the-box thinking"

"Noticed what?" I repeated.

"Feeling uncertain of your perceptions, frequently questioning if you are remembering things correctly, believing you are irrational or 'crazy'. Do I really need to remind you whose symptoms are they?"

"Gaslighting..." My mind supplied automatically, "But...by whom? Soovin or GG?"

Frank snapped his fingers, "That's a...good question. Why don't we come back to that later?"

"Then, as of now, 'Soovin is a liar' seems like the most rational conclusion to me," I said as I gave my cookies some final touches.

"Let's say he is, then...what are you planning to do, Han...?"

"I...I have no idea, Frank," I sighed.

"You do realize that if he is really willing to hand you in to his Mafia family or something, then, you can't live with that man, right?"

"I..." I was at a loss for words.

My brain and heart had drastically different plans and I was not in a condition to knock some sense into either of them.

"With GG being all 'I'll come' and 'Don't you worry about that', I don't think I would have to make this decision anytime soon. We will be pretty occupied in running around the world and trying to solve this matter"

"Come to think of it, how will we even solve this matter? Honestly, I don't see any way this ends well for us"

"Given the condition of our so-called 'team' right now, you should prefer some sugar-coating if you don't want our already fragmented team to break down. There is no need to be so frank, Frank"

I smiled at my own joke.

"Really? Be serious, Han!" He exclaimed.

"My bad," I muttered, "Right, so...the only comforting end I see to this is GG dying because that guy is not going to give up till his last breath...Or Soovin returning whatever it was that he wants but I highly doubt GG would be satisfied with that. He doesn't seem the kind of person who believes in forgive and forget"

"There is another way...if you are bold enough to walk on it..."

I frowned and looked at Frank. His face said it all.

"NO Frank, that is *not* happening," I screeched.

"Look, Han, it's just the fastest and the most practical solution, and if Soovin has indeed been a liar all along...I don't see anything fundamentally wrong with this"

"What about Anna?"

"She would be incredibly safe with him and we both know it"

"I...No, Frank. I am not *leaving* them behind. *Not a chance*"

"I am just saying," He held up his hands, "GG even offered to work together with you. I don't think he will hold a massive grudge against you. You did humiliate him but I think you can easily handle that. Of course, unless...you don't want to leave Anna...and Soovin"

I read his face, "I know what you are trying to do, Frank. You very well knew from the beginning I was not going to leave them, didn't you?"

"Hey," He smiled and shrugged, "I am just trying to make you realize what your sixth sense is saying. You have clouded it with details and practical solutions. But now, I think you know what your sixth sense, which has always been right may I remind you, actually says about this"

"You think Soovin meant it when he said GG had fed me a manipulated version of the story?" I looked at him.

"All I am saying is that you should at least give him a chance to explain what he thinks is happening. You can't judge anything without hearing both sides of the story, can you?"

I remained quiet as I pondered over it.

"Look, Han," He sighed, "I have seen his condition when you were in a coma. I am no Sherlock but I firmly believe that he didn't need to act *that* much for a stupid plan. It could be to win my trust, I know that but...Something about him makes me believe he really cares for you, despite what the recent facts point to. Remember what Mr. Dune always used to say? Facts can be deceiving but your sixth sense has the power to read true emotions..."

"Trust it over anything else..." I completed.

"You know I am an overprotective type of brother"

"Oh, I know that very well," I smiled.

"But if I had to give the responsibility of your protection to someone...it will be Soovin...and only him. Well, it could have been Wade as well when it comes to your protection but I really think he is out of the picture right now"

"It was not his fault, " I shook my head, "Life was devastatingly unfair to him. He *never* deserved what he got"

"I never said he did!" He held up his hands defensively, "I just don't fancy him and GG crossing paths even on accident. It...It will destroy the world, Han...You know that"

"I wish I didn't...I kind of miss the old times..." I stared into space reminiscing some of the memories we had together.

Suddenly, the oven beeped and I turned my attention to my freshly baked cookies, pushing those memories to the back of my mind.

"You two were close?" Frank asked.

I laughed, "We basically grew up together *and* worked together. Of course, we were! I wouldn't have risked my entire career for him if this wasn't the case, genius"

He reached for one of the cookies.

I smacked his hand, "They are hot, blondie!"

"So am I!" He smiled and devoured the cookie.

I shook my head at him disapprovingly but ate one as well.

"Delicious," I sighed deeply in content.

"Do you think Wade will try to reach you after saving Mr. Dune...?" Frank asked while taking another cookie.

"Knowing him, he will try his *absolute* best to"

"And...how good is that?" He tilted his head to one side.

I scoffed, "As good as the CIA and FBI *combined*"

"Oh, we are in *deep* trouble..." Frank grumbled, "The next thing you know he is banging on our door-"

Suddenly, there was a knock on the door.

CHAPTER TWENTY-SEVEN

Vanishing Cookies And People

"I take it back! I take it *back!*" Frank hissed while looking above as if some magical force would buy it and change our circumstances.

"If it's really him, Frank, I am going to tape your mouth," I said while reaching for my gun.

I advanced towards the door as my heartbeat fastened. I had no idea who or what to expect. So, I had prepared my mind accordingly. If you see someone with a gun, shoot first and think later.

I took a deep breath and shared a look with Frank who had already taken his fighting position as well.

Here goes nothing, I thought as I threw the door open and aimed my gun at whoever was standing outside the door.

"OH MY GOD, WHAT IS WRONG WITH YOU?!" Anna screamed in surprise when my gun was a millimetre away from her head.

I immediately pulled my gun back, "It's you..."

I sighed in relief, "And here we were, thinking it was...Never mind, what are you doing here?"

"I could ask you the same question," She replied, narrowing her eyes.

"I am an adult. I can roam around as I please," I replied.

She shook her head at me, "You never sleep, do you?"

"What are you doing here, Anna?" Frank asked.

She rounded on him, "What are *you* doing-"

"We asked you first!" We both scowled at the same time.

"Geez! Calm down, you both. I just couldn't find Dad anywhere and I was getting really bored," She came inside the room.

"Hold up," Frank said, "You were getting bored so you decided to roam about in this ancient hotel all by yourself at 3 AM, that too when the receptionist doesn't seem very fond of you?"

"Yes, but she is gone" She jumped over and sat on the counter, "And by the way, it's 4 AM. You guys have been up since 3 AM?"

"Han, I think it's about time you introduce your daughter to this really advanced concept of *common sense*"

"Wait," I said, "You said you couldn't find your Dad anywhere?"

"Yeah, I looked in my room and even your room but he wasn't there," She shrugged.

I and Frank exchanged a look.

Both our faces read, 'This is not good'.

"But he is also an *adult,* right Mom? So, I don't think he would get lost in the corridors or something," She smirked, "Why are both your faces so serious and frowned?"

"When did you see him last time?" Frank asked.

"Where did you see him last time?" I added.

"He was sleeping or rather pretending to be asleep on his bed till 11 PM"

"Pretending to be asleep?" Frank frowned.

"I know him. He wasn't asleep but acting as if he was"

"Why?" I wondered aloud.

She shrugged.

"More importantly," Frank interrupted my thoughts, "Where is he?"

"Hey!" Anna jumped off the counter, "Are those cookies?"

I exclaimed, "Be careful, Anna! They are hot-"

But she was already busy gobbling the cookies.

I shook my head at her as a smile appeared on my lips.

But then, the smile turned into a frown, *There should be three more cookies. Where did the rest go?*

"Okay," Frank said, "I know I am kind of dumb but I can swear there should be more cookies on that tray than what are left"

"The vanishing cookies are pretty good," Anna said.

"I am serious!" Frank exclaimed.

"Well, so am I," She shrugged in reply.

Frank turned to me and groaned, "How *do* you put up with this on a daily basis, Han?"

"You kind of accept your fate after the first year," I said sincerely.

"Hey! I think that was an insult," Ann frowned.

"Really? What makes you say that, Anna?" Frank said sarcastically.

She glowered at him and put another cookie in her mouth, not breaking the eye contact.

"That's enough cookies for you," I said and picked up the tray, holding it out of her reach.

"Mom," She groaned like a kid despite being fifteen years old, "I know those are Dad's favorite but I really think he wouldn't mind if I took one from his share. He loves me!"

I packed the cookies in a disposable container and handed it to her, "Give this to your Dad when you find him, okay?"

She barely held a smirk and side-eyed me, "I thought you were mad at him"

"I thought you were willing to make a conversation with you easy for once" I retorted back, trying my best not to blush.

"This brings us back to the question, where is that guy?" Frank said and shot me a Thank-me-later look.

I rolled my eyes. Being in a room with these two taking turns at pulling my leg was nothing short of a nightmare.

"I don't know," Anna shrugged, "As I told you, I have searched everywhere"

I looked at Frank. This was serious.

Anna looked at both of us and said, "Is it that serious...?"

Either Soovin had indeed lied to me about everything and was up to some devious scheme or...

"GG"

"Wade"

I and Frank said simultaneously.

"What does Wade have to do with this?" I asked, slightly irritated.

"It is entirely possible, Han. What if he somehow saw you both arguing on the street and decided to step in?" Frank tried to reason.

We both had started panicking.

"Okay," I held my hands up, "That does sound like something he would do but come on, Frank! GG being behind this is more possible. Just think about it!"

"You guys are drawing conclusions about him being abducted, has either of you thought that he wouldn't have gone with them easily without a fight?" Anna said casually but I could see her panicking as well.

"That's true but they both have their ways," Frank said.

"Like a sleeping pill in a cheeseburger," I added while cringing due to the nostalgia.

"Mom, what are you even talking about?" Anna frowned, "And if GG had come, do you really think he would have left all of us asleep?"

"Had he eaten anything, Anna?" I asked.

"No?" She said with a puzzled look.

"If they had used some drug in the air or an injection, Anna would have heard the commotion," Frank said.

"He wouldn't have gone with them without a fight..." I repeated to myself as the wheels of my brain began turning, "We would have heard him if he had struggled...THIS DOESN'T MAKE ANY SENSE!?"

"Who says somebody took him?" Frank said with wide eyes, "What if he went willingly?"

"That's ridiculous, Frank! Why would he go willingly...THE THING GG WANTED FROM HIM!" I exclaimed.

"You think he has gone to return that mystery object? But he had said that it wasn't with him!" Anna said.

"He could have bluffed," Frank suggested with a shrug.

"Gee...Soovin Cooper bluffing...Who could have thought that?" I smacked the countertop in frustration.

"But why would he return it all of a sudden if he has kept whatever that thing is with him for over five years?" Frank pulled at his hair.

"I can bet that he is doing something so stupid that we will never expect it..." I muttered.

"But where and what?" Anna exclaimed anxiously.

"Think, Han!" Frank exclaimed, "You are the one who knows him the most. Where could Soovin go at this time in a strange place he barely knows anything about?"

I shut my eyes and focused.

Where could he have gone?

He was mentally upset and possibly angry at me for thinking he would trade me and moreover, not giving him a chance to explain. He was blaming himself saying, 'No matter what I try to do...I just hurt people. That's all I am good at!'

He also wanted to know what GG had told me...

My eyes flew open as the picture became clear to me. The cookies...the sound...how could have I been that stupid?

I knew exactly where that adorable idiot was.

"SOOVIN COOPER, YOU BETTER NOT BE BEHIND THAT DAMN CURTAIN!?" I screamed and turned around.

I yanked the curtain away and there he was...standing with a cookie in his one hand and his gun in the other with cookie crumbs on his lips.

He smiled at me uncertainly, fully aware of the fact that I was ready to beat the pulp out of him for his stupidity.

Frank cursed loudly when Soovin became visible and Anna clutched at her heart in surprise, screaming, "DAD!?"

"Okay, let's be a bit civil about this..." He said with fear, "You guys are some real overthinkers, I must say..."

I thundered, "I AM GOING TO KILL YOU, YOU LITTLE-"

Suddenly the door of the pantry burst open and this time...the people were a lot more dangerous than Anna...

CHAPTER TWENTY-EIGHT

THE SUDDEN GUESTS

One second I was screaming at Soovin and the other, we were at the gunpoint of a dozen men with that wrecked tattoos on their arms.

Immediately, we all held out our guns and surrounded Anna who was defenceless, forming an outward shield around her.

"How the hell did they get to know our location?" Frank muttered while trying to point his gun at every single one of them.

"More importantly, why are they here?" Soovin asked frantically.

"I think we all know the answer to the why. The how on the other hand, is not going to save us from being shot," I replied as my mind worked frantically.

"Call Captain," The man in the center told the man who was standing right beside him.

So, he is the Boss of the group, I immediately put him at the aim of my gun and noticed Frank doing the same.

"I am not complaining or anything but why aren't they attacking us?" Frank said.

"They don't have the orders to," Soovin deduced.

"HELLO THERE!" GG's terrible voice boomed from a speaker held by one of his men.

"Really? A speaker?" Anna said in disbelief.

"A typical melodramatic eccentric villain," I muttered.

"I suppose you must be wondering how or rather why my men are here," GG said in a sing-song voice.

"Honestly, neither of us gives a damn about it anymore," Frank shouted at the speaker.

"Careful, Officer Frank," He said menacingly, "You are at the gunpoint of twelve of my men. A big mouth could prove to be lethal in this scenario"

"What do you want, Gavin?" Soovin gritted out.

"How many times do I need to tell you, Soovin?" All playfulness vanished from his voice as he said, "Return it"

"It was never yours," Soovin matched his tone.

"I am *making* it mine," GG rasped, "No matter if I have to step over the dead body of my old partner for it. Give it to me now and-"

"Let me guess. And you'll let us all go free?" Soovin laughed, "Amazing joke. None of us are falling for the oldest trick in the book"

"Oh, I was not going to say that," GG said playfully, "If you return it, you will be killed quickly and without much pain but if you don't...Let's just say I will let my men have some fun with you lot"

"We'll take the second option, then," I said, matching his confidence level, "After all, your men aren't the only people who know how to play"

"As confident as ever, Officer!" GG laughed, "But may I remind you, you are greatly outnumbered and I am not there for you to blackmail my men. So..."

"Coward," Anna muttered.

"WHAT DID YOU CALL ME, LITTLE ONE?!" He thundered.

"COWARD!" Anna shouted at him, "YOU ARE A COWARD WHO LOVES TO HIDE BEHIND HIS MEN BECAUSE THAT'S ALL HE IS CAPABLE OF!"

"Han, I really think you need to teach her about common sense," Frank said uneasily as GG's men started acting less like humans and more like chained hunting dogs who had just seen a prey.

"YOU WANT TO TEST MY PATIENCE? I CAN ORDER MY MEN TO TEAR YOU ALL APART-"

"Oh but can you?" Soovin smirked, "After all, I am the only one who can give you what you desperately need"

GG laughed and my skin tinged with a weird sensation.

"That's exactly what I mean, old friend. It's only *you* I need alive. Not Officer Frank, your pesky little daughter, or your sweet spot, Officer Hannah Gorgin. I can easily kill all of them if you don't give that to me. You *know* I can, Soovin"

The beads of sweat on Soovin's forehead were proof that he indeed knew that GG could and probably would do so.

"Give it back or everyone dies, you a bit later than the rest but surely," GG rasped.

Soovin remained quiet.

GG clicked his tongue, "I know that silence very well. You've made the wrong choice, bud...HOLD THEM DOWN, BOYS!"

All of his men lunged toward us and we started firing but there were too many people and way too skilled people. They knew very well how to use their shields as well as guns.

Slowly and steadily, they were surrounding us so that we had no place to go.

"We are going to run out of bullets like this!" I screamed while taking down one of the men.

"But *they* won't," Soovin gritted out, his remark aimed at the fact that each of them carried three guns and god knows how many clips.

"Exactly," I smiled with a spark of madness in my eyes, "They won't"

One of the men lunged towards us from behind the cover of the other two men. I shot him and instead of pushing him away, grabbed his guns and handed two of them to Frank and Soovin while taking the third one myself.

"They are gaining on us and there are still 9 of them left!" Soovin said while reloading his gun.

"Han, we are surrounded!" Frank exclaimed.

"Excellent," I said while firing like a caveman, "We can attack in any direction"

"I am scared!" Anna sobbed.

I and Soovin shared a look.

We could not let them touch Anna, no matter what.

"They are tightening the circle," Frank reported, "We don't stand a chance against them if we stick together like this. They will simply aim all the firepower at one place"

"Soovin, you'll be with Anna. I'll give you temporary cover. No arguments," I said, "Separate on the count of three"

Soovin muttered, "At least someone finally remembers my name"

"One," I said, concentrating only on staying alive.

"Two," Soovin said.

"Three!" Frank exclaimed.

"SEPARATE!" I screamed.

Soovin scooped up Anna and jumped behind the counter. I shot at the guy obstructing his path. He dodged the bullet but had to move away for his dear life.

"HAN, WE ARE FINE. TAKE COVER!" Soovin screamed from behind the counter.

I used a large box of goods that was lying on the floor as a cover. From my peripheral view, I saw Frank peeking from behind another such box.

"THEY HAVE HEAVY FIRE POWER!?" He screamed over the deafening gunshots.

I looked at Frank and mouthed, 'Let's go for the leader'

He nodded and signalled, 'One...Two...Three'

We both surged forward without any cover and made a run for the leader. By this time, I had deduced that making the leader a hostage was impossible in the midst of this war zone. Taking him down was our only hope.

We located him standing alone behind his shield and shooting well-thought and considerate shots. We looked at each other and nodded.

Frank threw himself over the skinny leader, tackling him to the ground, and immediately rolled away from him. I took the clear shot and when the guy's eyes closed, they didn't open again.

However, none of the men seemed to be even slightly dazed by that. They were ready to die fighting or more probably, kill their opponents in the worst way possible without thinking about their or their teammate's lives.

We both ducked behind a pillar.

"The plan failed," Frank panted, "What now?"

"I-"

My eyes widened as I saw Anna and Soovin being held by two giants at gunpoint, "We need to save them, Frank"

"They will get us for sure," Frank replied while taking some shots.

"We need to try. They will get us anyway," I shrugged.

"But...why are they holding them down? They literally have a clear shot"

"Their orders were to hold us down...not kill us," My eyes widened with realization, "They won't kill us until GG has not told them to"

"Well, then," Frank reloaded his gun, "I guess we can go all banshees on them because we literally cannot do anything else"

"Let's take down as many men as possible before they capture us, at least," I told him as we both got out of the cover and started firing.

This technique took one of their men down before we both were captured as well and made to stand beside Soovin and Anna as they waited for GG to get on line.

"Ah, I see you all have done your job," He said.

"Yes, Captain," They all replied in perfect sync.

"What happened to that sharp tongue, Officer?" He sneered.

"Oh, don't worry. It's still sharp enough to slice through your inflated ego, you meathead!" I shouted at the speaker.

"Aww...is that desperation I hear?" GG said playfully, "No worries, let me free you from it! Point the gun at her"

Within a fraction of a second, six people had pointed twelve guns right at my head.

I gulped, *Well, this could have gone better.*

"Soovin," GG rasped, "Tell me where it is, *right now* or she dies"

"I...I can't!" Soovin screamed in desperation.

"Load," GG said.

His men were quick to follow his instructions.

"Gavin, wait-" Soovin tried to stop him.

"Three," He cut him off in a rather nonchalant way.

"Let's-"

"Two"

I could see his men place their fingers on the trigger, ready to pull it the second GG said attack, and all I could do was clench my eyes shut and accept my fate.

I could hear his smirk when he said, "One"

CHAPTER TWENTY-NINE

THE KEY TO PROJECT 12

"YOU CAN'T ACCESS IT WITHOUT HER!" Soovin screamed desperately, "SHE NEEDS TO BE ALIVE TO OPEN IT!"

GG laughed, "Now, who is trying to fool someone with the oldest trick in the book? You expect me to believe that?"

Soovin's eyes narrowed, "Does Project 12 ring a bell?"

I could hear GG gasp.

I let out a breath I didn't know I was holding, *I am not dying today.*

"That project failed! You had no idea how to make it work," GG said but his voice seemed hollow.

"I had quite a lot of time after that, didn't I?" Soovin smirked.

"No, you didn't! It must have taken ages even if you did manage to make it work!" GG started panicking.

"Oh, the time was enough!"

"Even if it is true, why would you make *her* the key? Anna would obviously be your first choice"

"Well, if you think so..." He said with a smug face, "Go ahead, take your chances"

GG took a deep breath, "Boys-"

"Just remember that," Soovin smiled as if he knew he had won this battle of words, "You will *never* get your hands on it if you do this. Don't say I didn't warn you, old friend"

"Point the gun at the girl," GG ordered in spite and his men followed.

Soovin didn't seem even slightly bothered.

He simply shrugged, "Or I could have indeed chosen Anna"

GG shouted, "WHO DID YOU CHOSE?!"

"Or..." Soovin's smirk widened, "I could have toyed a bit with the system and made sure that more than one person was required to access it. Who knows? Maybe I even added Frank to the list?"

"Now, why on Earth would you add *Frank* there?"

"I don't know," He shrugged mockingly, "Maybe because I knew you would not expect that. I have always been two steps ahead of you in technological stuff, remember?"

GG laughed, "I am such an idiot! I almost forgot! You had chosen the project's key before you met our lovely Officer Hannah"

Soovin acted confident but I could see the panic in his eyes, "Oh, you think so? I did have enough time to change that, may I remind you"

Meanwhile, my mind was working on weakening his men because I had long ago given up on making any sense of their talk.

My thought process had never been faster, *They have firepower on their side but they are essentially idiots. They follow whatever GG orders them without any questions or any thinking. Confusion is the only thing that can be on our side, right now.*

"You know what? I am willing to take the chances now," GG said and I saw Soovin flinch.

Of course, GG had been quick to catch the tone of Soovin's voice.

I looked at Soovin's desperate face. He had no other plan to buy us any time.

Think quickly, Gorgin, I pumped myself.

GG continued with his mundane monologue, "I almost feel sorry for you Officer. Come to think of it, your fault is little to none but what can I do now? Nothing is more pathetic than a CIA Officer without a team to back her up or an organization to help her, is there?"

I snorted back as a plan formed in my mind, "How about a psychopath without his pack of dogs? Or even better a confused pack of dogs without their leader for ordering them around and guiding their every basic move?"

Before GG could say anything, I kicked the man holding me between the legs and shot at the speaker which sparked and died within a second.

Then, all hell broke loose.

Frank and Soovin caught up with me, freed themselves, and helped Anna to knock out the man holding her.

We all together hid behind the long counter as GG's men started shooting uncertainly without any sense of direction. They had no idea what to do because they no longer had any orders.

"There are six of them left now," Soovin panted, "We might actually make it out alive. There is like a 10% chance"

"Thanks a lot for the words of encouragement, Dad!" Anna scowled.

"Hey, you are not supposed to lie or sugarcoat during a shoot-out. Besides, this is a damn good chance," He replied while occasionally peeking out of the cover to fire some random shots, "Man, these ones are tougher than the rest"

"They are trying to find another way to connect with GG," I reported, "We need to use this short distraction to knock out as many men as possible"

"On it," Frank said while taking some more shots, "One more down. Five left"

I said after around five minutes of us shooting like that, "Only four left"

"Make that three," Soovin smiled while taking another man down.

"What did you do that for?" GG's voice boomed, earning a groan from all of us, "Now, you owe me $130, Officer"

"No worries, I'll pay you in bullets and insults, you nit-wit," I gritted out while trying to get a clear shot but now that the connection had been restored, all the men were back in laser-focus mode, making it a near impossible task.

"Listen, boys. I need all of them alive. If you beat then till they pass out, it is fine with me but they should be breathing," GG said to his men, "You all are way more in number-"

"Actually, they are all outnumbered right now if Anna counts," I said smugly.

"THERE IS ONLY THREE OF YOU LEFT!?" GG shrieked.

"Yes, Captain," replied the uncertain men like trained robots.

"You know what? I don't care. You all are among my best men. Even three of you are enough. Just bring them to me," He said.

This was met with another round of 'Yes, Captain' from the three bulky men as the line went dead.

"Oh, good luck with that," Frank said, smiling as he shot at one of the three remaining men.

"Darn it!" He muttered when the guy blocked it with ease, "Okay, maybe we are the ones who need luck on our side"

"Well, aren't you quick enough to figure that out?" I said sarcastically while shooting blindly at them.

"We need to do something different or we will definitely run out of bullets," Soovin said while reloading his gun.

"Okay, listen. I'll jump out of the cover. Their aim will be on me. Take advantage and shoot," I said, getting ready.

"YOU ARE NOT JUMPING OUT OF THE COVER!" Soovin shouted.

"You are lucky that the shots are loud or they would have heard you and I would have killed you for ruining my plan," I replied.

"Han, I really think-" Frank tried to talk.

"Now!" I interrupted him and jumped out from behind the counter towards the box that had earlier served as my cover.

This worked and they were able to knock out one man.

I peeked around and noticed the two men sharing a look. One of them reloaded while the other nodded at him.

"This is their last clip," I said to myself, "They are going to try something different too"

Before I knew it, one of the men rushed towards me. He threw the large box that was acting like my cover away as if it was made of paper and lunged towards me.

I jumped back in surprise and barely managed to shoot him in time.

My eyes widened as their plan dawned on me but it was as usual, too late.

The other guy held his gun at the back of my head, "Make a move and you get shot"

"You don't have the orders to kill me," I said calmly but froze as he had suggested.

"We both know that I can shoot you at a dozen places for you to not die, just faint," He muttered menacingly, still maintaining distance from me, probably because he knew that that way, he could stay away from my attacks and have enough time to shoot me and dodge if I decided to pull off any stunts, "Don't move a muscle"

Given his intelligence, I chose wisely to comply with him.

"COME OUT OR SHE DIES!" He screamed while taking a step away from me.

He is trying to keep all of us at the gun's point. He is really clever, I thought.

All of them came out from behind the counter slowly, completely ignoring me as I screamed, "STAY HIDDEN, YOU IDIOTS!"

Soovin was ahead of them both and Frank was busy forcing Anna to stay hidden behind him.

"Make one funny move and I'll press the trigger," The guy said.

"So will we," Soovin replied with his gun pointed steadily at the man behind me.

"Oh, how about now?" I heard him move.

Soovin's gun followed his movement until it was pointed right at me.

I noticed Soovin's grip loosen as sweat covered his palms.

Despite knowing that he wouldn't shoot me, looking at him with his gun pointed directly at me made my skin crawl as if one of my nightmares had come true.

He gave me a stiff, barely visible nod and I knew exactly what it meant.

I mouthed, 'Three...Two...One'

I ducked below as Soovin's shot echoed off the walls. I had almost relaxed when I heard the man's laugh.

"I am not naive," He hissed out, "What did I say about any funny move?"

His voice seemed closer.

I flinched as I suddenly felt his hands grip my wrists behind my back.

Soovin's entire demeanour changed and his bright eyes seemed darker all of a sudden. His face showed a chilling amount of rage.

He gritted out in a way that gave even me the urge to clench my eyes shut, "You touch her...and I will make you learn *exactly* what is worse than death"

I heard the man gulp.

His confident voice trembled a bit when he said, "I have the upper hand here, hero. I can kill her if I want to"

But I could hear him step away from me as if I was making him uneasy or rather...*Soovin was.*

"Technically you can," Soovin said with his eyes fixed at the guy, his gaze dripping with inhumanely cold contempt, "I of all people know what GG will do to you in that case but...I assure you what *I* will do to you...would make him seem like a god...*I promise*"

I shivered from head to toe even though I knew he was not talking to me. Even Frank and Anna looked uncomfortable. I could only imagine how that guy must be feeling.

"Well," his voice was quaking, "If I am going to die anyway...I'll take her with me"

I turned around only to see him pressing the trigger...with his gun pointed right at my head...

The worst part?

I couldn't even move in that half a second, because then, the bullet would hit Soovin.

So, I remained frozen as the bullet made its way towards me...

CHAPTER THIRTY

A Letter From A Friend

"HAN!?" Soovin screamed and before I could process what was happening, he leaped towards me, pushing me away and getting himself on the target of the bullet in the process.

I reflexively pushed him away; his body twisted a bit and the bullet hit him an inch below his heart.

"SOOVIN!?" I let out an involuntary scream as he fell to the floor, carried by momentum.

I was dimly aware of Frank shooting the guy's arm, the guy running away and Frank chasing after him with Anna at his heels.

All I could focus on was how quickly blood was soaking Soovin's white shirt.

My hands trembled as I examined the wound and looked hither and tither frantically to find a first-aid kit. On not finding any near me, I ripped apart the sleeve of my shirt and did the best I could.

"It's gonna hurt, Soovin," I looked at him as I got ready to apply the pressure.

He only hummed in response; his eyes were busy staring fondly at me.

I took a deep breath and applied the necessary pressure.

He flinched slightly.

"It's just an inch below your heart," I said while trying my best to be gentle.

He just stared at me wordlessly.

I avoided his gaze, "How did you know the bullet would hit you below the heart and not right on it?"

His eyes never left my face, "I didn't"

"Then, why did you jump in front of me? You could have-"

He softly lifted my chin and my teary-eyed gaze met his soft one, "You still think I am doing all of this to trade you to my family for some money...?"

"I..." My voice grew thick.

I looked into his eyes and knew the answer.

"No, Soovin...I should not have-"

"It's not your fault, Han," He said softly, "I of all people know what GG can do to your mind...and my history with trust has not been the best...That phone call...I should've told you about it and explained it instantly...If I was in your place, I would have done the same thing"

I let out a hollow scowl as my lips split into a smile, "How much of my conversation did you eavesdrop on?"

He smiled in return, "More than you would like...But I still have to know about that *son of Mr. Dune*"

My gaze diverted to his chest, "How about we get that wound properly treated first? Then, we can both take turns at explaining"

"Oh, I'll live," He winked at me and I could feel the entire zoo in my stomach, "Not gonna lie, I kind of missed you calling me by my name and I am still looking forward to a deeply felt apology by you"

I could feel his breathing getting laboured, "You are getting up or not? Also, stop hiding the pain with a smile. I have been shot multiple times. I know how much it hurts"

"Damn, right. It hurts like hell," He groaned in pain, "But...are we good now?"

"Yes, you idiot. Now, come on," I smiled and gently offered him my arm.

I helped him up just as Frank came into the room with Anna.

He panted, "Is he fine?"

"The wound isn't too bad but we need to remove the bullet," I replied while carrying Soovin whose arm was around my shoulder for support.

"Let's lay him down in one of the rooms. I bought a first-aid kit from the chemist down the block on my way back"

"You got him?"

"Ya, I shot him and threw him away in the nearest dumpster," He shrugged, "But we need to get out of here before that old lady arrives. She is not going to be happy with the mess we have made and all these bodies lying here and there"

I took a deep breath only after the bullet had been removed from Soovin's chest and his wound had been properly treated.

"It will still take a lot of time to heal," I told him.

"Oh, I am good," He waved his hand dismissively.

I shook my head at him while smiling.

"So, you both are no longer at each other's throats?" Anna asked smiling.

We both turned towards her to roll our eyes and scowl but my eyes noticed something else.

"Anna, what's that in your hand?" I asked.

"Oh, I almost forgot," She stretched out her hand for me to take it, "This letter was on the reception desk. It is addressed to Dad"

"A letter in the 21st century?" I raised my eyebrows as I examined it.

Soovin laughed, "That's ridiculous-"

Suddenly, he stopped mid-laugh and his eyes widened, "Oh no..."

"You good, bro?" Frank asked.

All Soovin's eyes showed was fear, "Han, don't..."

I raised my eyebrows questioningly at him.

He gulped, "You *can* read it...Just...Give me a chance to explain before drawing conclusions...Promise that you'll listen to me"

"I am getting a feeling we will *not* like it..." Frank muttered as he looked at the letter in my hand with distaste.

"Soovin, that's-"

"It's going to look really bad, Han. Just...Promise me you will hear me out, no matter what happens, PLEASE!"

"Fine, I promise!" I narrowed my eyes, *this couldn't be good.*

"My experience with letters and notes left at doorsteps and receptions haven't been good anyway," I muttered as I unfolded the letter.

My heart stopped and tears filled my eyes as I finished reading it. The letter flew away with a strong gust of wind but I stood rooted to the spot, frozen in time.

I heard Soovin calling me, "HAN, LISTEN TO ME! YOU PROMISED YOU WOULD HEAR ME OUT NO MATTER WHAT!?"

Anna's voice seemed close yet distant, "HOW COULD HAVE YOU DONE THIS, DAD?!"

Frank's screams were dulled with my heartbeat deafening me, "I WAS THE ONE WHO TOLD HER TO LISTEN TO YOU, YOU RASCAL!? DO YOU EVEN KNOW THE VALUE OF TRUST?!"

However, Soovin seemed to be staring at only me, "YOU PROMISED, HAN...PLEASE GIVE ME ONE MORE CHANCE..."

I clenched my jaw and finally met his desperate gaze. I felt my anger snatch the reigns of control from my mind.

Within a second, I took out my gun and held it at his forehead.

Soovin gulped and said, "You promised to listen to me, Han..."

I gritted out as tears streamed down my face, "And you swore that it was all a misunderstanding..."

Then, before he could open his mouth and blind me with another one of his sweet lies...I pulled the trigger...

～

You are doing great, Soovin. I have been keeping a watch and I am thoroughly impressed that you managed to convince Hannah Gorgin that you do care about her even after Gavin almost ruined everything. All is going according to the plan. It's perfect, son.

Still, we cannot overlook that you have failed to hand her over at the hospital, Soovin. Your mother is infuriated by that failure and wishes to punish you rather brutally. I have tried my best to tell her that if it was not for GG, Hannah would have been here with us as a hostage.

In the end, because you are still our son, I have managed to talk your mother into giving you one last chance but she is not ready to let you go without any punishment. It is a miracle in itself that I have convinced her for this deal...Bring Hannah Gorgin, her brother, and that little girl Anna to our cabin in Norway and kill them all as I have already said in the message I had sent to you. Your mother says that they are not worth any more time and you have lost your chance to start a family with that girl.

Kill them all and come home, your mom has got one job for you that will help you prove yourself for the final time and if you fail...you will meet the same fate...

Your father,
Arnold Cooper

～

About The Author

DrishKing or Drishti Ummat is a high schooler with a burning passion for writing books. She is a true bookworm, always trying to read as many books as possible. Somehow, that high schooler got interested in writing books. Her love for writing fuels her self-publishing. She is an introvert who despises reality and lives in her own world, which is filled with horrors, mystery, and humor.

Although not published, she has written quite a few books and is slowly editing and publishing them as e-books, paperbacks, hardcovers, and everything else you can ask for.

She currently lives with her family in Bathinda, Punjab.

The author can be contacted via - E-mail: drishtiummat@gmail.com

Books By The Author

Guilty Or Not...?: Secrets Of A Wanted Criminal

Will justice be served to all the families he had destroyed or to the family he was desperate to make?

CIA Officer Hananah Gorgin, the most skilled in her field, is working on a case involving the murder of Henry Spark alongside her engineer brother, Frank, who is fascinated by her work. The investigation leads the unusual duo to the infamous assassin Soovin Cooper, the only criminal Hannah has been unable to put behind bars.

However, when Hannah discovers Soovin's secret, she questions his guilt. This realization causes Hannah to reevaluate her feelings towards Soovin, and she even contemplates leaving her life behind to be with the pseudo-assassin and a little girl.

She finds herself torn between her duty and her emotions.

But the question remains - Is Soovin truly ready to leave his violent past behind? Furthermore, is this all a mere sinister plot for him or something deeper? And most importantly - Is Soovin guilty or not...?

Guilt Unfolds: The Ghoul Of His Past

"Revenge is a dish best served cold"

Ex-CIA Officer Hannah Gorgin and ex-Assassin Soovin Cooper had forgotten their past and were living their best life with their daughter Anna when a gift from an old friend turns their life upside down - A package and a note stained with blood.

Turns out, Soovin wasn't all innocent...

Their pasts are catching up, can they run fast enough or will the buried truth resurface...?

An unlikely match in a relationship based upon lies, will they give up?

"Promise?"

"Promise"

The White Face Man: Horrors Of A Mirror

What will you do when you don't see your reflection in the mirror and are instead presented with a heart-stopping murder that will give you never-ending nightmares? Moreover, it ends with a message written in blood - 'YOU ARE NEXT'

The White Face Man isn't the devourer of just one soul. His victims push others into this whirlpool in hopes of escaping but The White Face Man shows no mercy and slaughters everyone.

"I am Cari Hallen, one of his victims. I remember thinking I had escaped as well This is my encounter with The White Face man. Lucky are the ones who haven't witnessed his

horrors. Beware, now, whenever you see a mirror, you will recall a white mask and a blood-stained knife."

But can an emotionless being like The White Face Man be humane too? After all a villain is just a victim whose story hasn't been told, right?

The Curse Of KV-62: Provoking The Boy King

This is the story of -
A troubled past and a lethal curse,
A burning passion for tombs and a thousand little secrets,
Hunger for answers and an impossible mystery to solve,
Courage to break a centuries-old curse and a promise to keep with the last breath

A renowned archaeologist and Egyptologist, Ken Hudson, the tomb of Tutankhamun or KV-62, and the curse of the boy king.

After seven years of research on tombs, Ken Hudson finally got the opportunity to scrutinize the tomb of Tutankhamun, or KV 62 with his friend Clark Limberdon. He has already lost his father to the same tomb but has plucked up the courage to unveil the mystery behind his father's demise and the tomb's rumored curse.

However, when he comes across a spine-chilling, dark, prophetic note written by his father for him about the tomb, his objectives change. Now, instead of just finding the secret room in KV 62 he has been given the responsibility to uncover, he is going to cross the line and provoke the ancient forces.

Little did he know that The Tomb Of Tutankhamun was ready to take another life with it.

Join Ken Hudson in his magical adventure in The Tomb Of Tutankhamun, fighting the curse of KV-62.

Detective Wilbur Horace: A Case That Changed His Life

Detective Wilbur Horace - a detective with a little secret- is caught between three murders. The killer is overconfident for a reason, he is a true mastermind. Words like genius define him. He is leaving behind hints in the form of notes for the detective to catch up with his intelligence. But Wilbur Horace is a mastermind himself and he is the only one who can match the intelligence of the killer.

In fact, he is similar to the killer in countless ways, with similar habits, similar styles, and even the same blood group.

Will Wilbur be able to uncover the mystery behind the killings while hiding his little secret...? Will the killer get away with all the three murders he has committed? Or will Wilbur be able to decode the clues left behind, and put him behind bars? Or will this case take an unexpected turn so that neither of that happens, both of them lose and both of them somehow win in this face-off...?

Join Detective Wilbur on this case to find out...

A True Mastermind-JJ: What Happens When An Author Has To Save Not A Character's Life But Her Own?

It had been really easy to put my book's characters into lethal situations and take risks that could either end their lives or save them, but trust me, it's a lot more difficult to make such decisions when life at sake isn't of a fictional character, but yours.

I am a successful crime-fiction author, Jamie Jennifer or JJ, as I am usually called. I lead a pretty normal life. My biggest problem can be a deadline for work but nothing more serious until a psycho killer kidnaps me and wants to kill me in front of my fans, apparently to get 'famous'.

I have to use my mind, which has developed a lot by writing crime fiction, to get out of his range, that too alive.

Join me on this life-changing adventure of mine...

3 AM Poetry: Dealing With Ups And Downs Of Life

Sometimes, tears can't express the amount of pain a smile can hide, and ear-piercing cries for help can't contain the emotions silence conceals. But...no matter how far you have run in the wrong direction, no matter how deep you are sinking in a world of darkness and negativity, you always have the choice to get up and get your life together.

Wondering how to deal with ups and downs of life or questioning why should you even get up after every fall?

You are not alone. On this hard journey of building yourself up, these soul-touching poems have gotten your back.

Poetry is the outcome of strong emotions, buried feelings, innovative ideas, and unpopular opinions.

You can either walk through hell with a smile or crawl your way through hell while cursing your rotten luck.

All in all, the way you tackle problems and whether you bounce back when life smacks you down or not is what makes the difference.

These poems guide you and teach you how to deal with the ups and downs of life.

Let's jump right into an endless sea of depressive ideas with a seabed of motivation, inspiring you to jump up, get above those waves, and remember what it actually feels like to breathe freely again.

Whether it be the ups or downs of life, or somewhere in between, these fifty poems have got your back in portraying every emotion.

Downloading a free sample of the book to judge the quality of the poems is a step you are free to take.

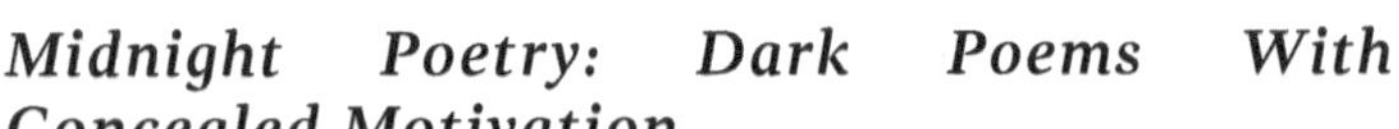

Midnight Poetry: Dark Poems With Concealed Motivation

Life isn't a bed of roses but more like a Ferris wheel. Ups and downs are an inevitable part of life. At times, one might ask himself why he should get up after a fall when all that is waiting for him is misery and more obstacles to face. At those times, he needs to get up and stand as strong as a mountain, ready to embrace the upcoming difficulties like a warrior.

This poem collection having fifty hand-picked poems explores the dark thoughts one might get in such hard times and help him to get up after every blow of life. These dark poems with concealed motivation enlighten issues that you might relate to or might be suffering through. Relating to a piece of writing and getting a sense of being understood when you think that you are the only one suffering can do wonders on a mind drowning in negativity.

'Not too many things feel greater than being understood'

And a poem is a thing that can be enjoyed by multiple people with different likings. From an old person to a little kid, we all enjoy reciting poems.